FLAMES

THE PHOENIX PROPHECY
BOOK FIVE

CARA CLARE

Flames
Copyright © 2022 Cara Clare.

The moral rights of the author have been asserted.
All rights reserved.

No part of this book may be reproduced, stored in a retrieval system, or transmitted in any form or by any means, electronic, mechanical, photocopying, recording, or otherwise, without the prior written permission of the publisher or copyright holder, except in the case of brief quotations embodied in critical articles or reviews.

This edition first published in Great Britain in 2025 by **Arcane Passion Press, an imprint of A.P Beswick Publications.**

Publishing rights are held by **A.P Beswick Publications** under license from the author.

ISBN (Paperback): 978-1-916671-71-3
ISBN (Hardback): 978-1-916671-72-0

A.P Beswick Publications
Oswaldtwistle Mills Business Centre, Clifton Mill, Pickup Street, Accrington, BB5 0EY
Cover Design: Beautiful Book Covers by Ivy

THE PHOENIX PROPHECY SERIES

Book One: Nova
Book Two: Blaze
Book Three: Ashes
Book Four: Embers
Book Five: Flames
Book Six: Fire Bird
Book Seven: Blood
Book Eight: Ice
Book Nine: Snow

Prequel novella: Hollow

Books 1-6 can be read as a complete story arc.
Books 7-9 follow Nova and the guys as they face a new threat.

When above turns to darkness
And below breaks free
A witch born to humans
Salvation shall bring
Fated to five who are not what they seem
The Phoenix will rise and become Earth's Queen
Into the embers
One
Two
Three
Devoured by Flame
The Phoenix is She

1

NOVA

For one long, quivering moment, everything goes black. My racing heartbeat fills my ears. Embers ignite in the pit of my being. They snake up through my body, filling the cracks between my bones—every sinew and every fiber.

When my eyes snap open, sounds come rushing back. Sam's voice echoes in the air, bouncing off the outer walls of the mansion, hanging in the trees, bleeding into my skin.

But he is gone.

Like a rapidly healing wound, the deep slash that swallowed him is closing. Kayla scrambles away from it. Briefly, a look of triumph crosses her face. Then she remembers; she attacked Sam because Nico sacrificed himself to save Sam's life.

Nico is gone too. She is now a mother without a child.

In an instant, Kayla is no longer human. She's a wolf. Sitting back on her haunches, she howls up at the hazy night sky above us. The sound of her distress catches on the fire that's growing inside me and, like lighter fuel, enflames it. I let out a roar. It rattles my rib cage and drowns out her howling. She looks at me, takes in my arms and legs—still bound by Eve's spell—then flees for the woods.

The rest of the werewolves have shifted too. They're gathered in a baying pack, guarding the fountain as Ragnor lowers his corpse bride into the water.

I turn my gaze on Eve. She is waving her arms, fluttering her fingers against her chest, singing words I don't understand.

Kole and the others are yelling at one another, desperately trying to free themselves from Eve's spell—but it's no use. As powerful as they are, they're helpless against her.

I am too. Powerless to escape.

As grief swirls through me, I screw my eyes shut again. Sam's face is all I can see. A sob escapes my lips. The fire is fading. My body folds in half as searing, visceral pain grips my insides.

"Nova," Luther's voice breaks through. "Find the fire. Latch onto it. Don't let it overwhelm you, but don't let it go. *Use* it."

"Nova, we're here." Mack's voice finds me too. "It's going to be alright."

"Nova, we'll get him back." Tanner sounds hoarse—like he's barely able to speak through the emotion that's circling him.

Little Star, you can free us. Only you. Kole's dark tone fill my head.

Only me... only me.

I slow my breathing. I ignore whatever the fuck is going on over at the fountain. Ragnor can have his zombie bride; that's of no concern to me now. I need Eve. I need her dead.

Before the fire can fade completely, I capture it. I picture it flickering back to life, licking my insides, becoming an inferno inside me. The flames grow and heat moves like liquid glass through my veins. This time, when I open my eyes, I'm on fire.

White hot flames have engulfed my arms, my hands, my body, my legs. Eve's eyes lock onto me. She tilts her head and stops singing, then she stumbles backward like something has barreled into her stomach and knocked her off balance. I flex my fingers then my toes. My muscles burn with the need to move. With a yell that makes the wolves fall silent and the fountain shudder, I bend Eve's restraining spell and pull my arms up in front of me.

Eve's eyes widen. She seems almost impressed. She watches as I rise to my feet. It's like moving through concrete. I tremble with the effort of it, but slowly I rise. Finally standing, with one last cry, I fling my arms to my sides and feel the invisible restraints snap like overstretched elastic.

Flames fall from my limbs, peppering the ground with sparks.

For a second, Eve simply stares at me, but then she nods at the wolves and shouts, "Seize her!"

They hesitate. They're scared of me but when Ragnor echoes Eve's request, they come for me. I turn on them and smile as they race across the small expanse of lawn between us. When they reach the scarred earth which marks the place Sam disappeared, I throw a wall of fire at them.

It comes forth like a tidal wave. Scorching hot air and tall orange flames roll toward the wolves. A couple are hit. They yelp and scramble backward. The rest are trapped. Casting a forcefield of fire around myself, I walk until I am just a few steps away from them and all that separates us are my flames.

"What are you waiting for?! Seize her and the fire will die!" Eve screeches.

I turn to her and cock my head. "Why don't you come get me yourself?" I ask.

Eve's eyes flicker. With her arms outstretched, she floats toward me like a harbinger of death. "You're going to regret asking that, Fire Bird," she sings.

"I don't think so," I mutter as I roll a ball of fire in her direction. She rises up and avoids it, but I send another, and another, and another. Finally, one catches her. In an instant, her clothes are alight. She tries to put them out, but I don't let her.

Eve tilts her head back and screams. As she does, movement catches the corner of my eye. They're free—my mages are free.

There's a flash of white and then Snow releases a roar that shakes me to my core. He thunders toward Eve while Kole pulls roots from the ground and binds her ankles. Luther rushes to my side. Tanner too. I let down my shield of fire and take each of their hands.

"Want to Johnny these wolves?" Luther asks, raising his eyebrows at me.

The image of Johnny's foul, loathsome body exploding from the inside out fills my head. "Try and stop me," I reply.

Together, we stride toward my wall of flames. The wolves are trapped. They have nowhere to go. Behind them, Ragnor is still in the fountain, clutching Elena's soaking-wet corpse to his chest. "Do not let them pass!" he yells. "Stop them!"

"You take the fountain," I tell Tanner, flicking my eyes from him to Ragnor. "We'll take the wolves."

Tanner squeezes my hand briefly. I open a window in the flames and let him pass. A wolf lunges for him, and then we do it. At the exact same moment, Luther and I tighten our grip on each other. The flames disappear. The wolves shudder and yelp. They howl. The smell of singed fur fills the air. More howling and then... BOOM.

Pieces of wolf fly through the air. Some splatter the walls

of the mansion. Some litter the earth. Some land in the fountain, filling it with gunk, and slime, and blood.

Ragnor stands up. Elena drips in his arms. "Help us! Why aren't you helping us?!" he yells at the sky. "Dark King, you must stop her. Stop The Phoenix!"

Tanner is at the side of the fountain now. He lifts his arms and pulls the water from it, sending it sloshing over the sides and flooding the ground, washing away remnants of wolf. Ragnor's eyes widen, he drops back to his knees and clutches Elena close, stroking her face. Tanner presses his fingers to his temples. My eyes narrow. I watch as he steps slowly forward, and Ragnor looks up.

"You want to know what hell feels like?" Tanner growls.

"What's he doing?" I look at Luther. He glances from me to Tanner as if he's unsure whether he should be letting this happen. Then at the exact same moment that Eve's screams fill the air, thunder booms above us. The slash of lightning is back, ripping open the sky. There's another clap of thunder. A sharp gasp comes from the direction of the fountain.

By the time I turn to look, Ragnor is no longer staring at a dead body. He holds a woman in his arms—a woman with long dark hair, pale skin, and wide eyes. She is still gasping for breath as if she's just surfaced from the bottom of the ocean. Eyes wide, she grabs Ragnor's shoulders, pulling at him with her long fingers.

"It's alright, my love, you're safe. You're safe," he whispers.

Staring at them, Tanner stumbles back and grabs his head. He cries out, and Luther catches him. "Tanner?" he asks. "Tanner? What is it?"

Ragnor is climbing out of the fountain. "Eve! Inside!" he yells at her and begins to run.

"No—" I lunge for him. "I'm not letting him go." I'm about to do to him what I did to the wolves when I catch Elena's face. A moment ago, she didn't exist but now she's here, and she didn't ask for any of this, and she's Sam's *mother*. She's terrified of me, clinging onto Ragnor like he's her valiant protector and I'm the evil witch trying to kill them.

I stop, wavering on the spot.

Behind us, another of Eve's screams fills the air. Bright white light, coming from the hole in the sky, is pummeling into her body. "He's filling me up," she cries. "The Shadow King is filling me up."

"The roots won't hold her," Kole shouts. He's running toward me, Snow at his side. "We need to get out of here."

He stops and looks at Tanner, who's still doubled over, hands gripping his head. Kole slips his arm around Tanner's waist and pulls him. "We have to go, Tanner. Now."

I can't move. Ragnor is on the steps, carrying Elena back inside. Bloody pieces of wolf decorate his hair and face. Hers too.

"We'll have another chance," Luther says as the ground begins to rumble beneath us and the sky flickers. "This isn't our moment."

"The Shadow King is coming," Eve yells then—just like that—the white light disappears, and the sky is zipped shut. She turns toward us. Her eyes are nothing more than pools of darkness in her gaunt face. She ticks her head to the side, then opens her mouth. This time, as she screams, a torrent of blackness comes flying out of her. It winds up into the air like smoke, but then I realize it isn't smoke; it's flies. Thousands of swarming black flies that keep coming and coming.

"Run." Luther grabs my hand. "Run! Now!"

2

SAM

At first, there's no pain. One second, I'm staring at Nova, reaching for her, desperately digging my nails into the cold earth, trying to stay with her. The next second, I'm falling.

Above me, the ground seals itself back up. The light disappears. There is only blackness. Blackness and the sensation of falling.

I don't land on anything. Instead, my whole body jolts—the way it does when you're on the cusp of sleep and are pried away from it. My eyes try to adjust to the light but there is nothing to adjust to. It's as if I'm suspended in emptiness. Miles and miles of nothing presses down on me, squeezing the air from my lungs.

I can't even see my own body. I run my hands over my arms. They still exist. *I* still exist.

"Is this death?" My voice echoes in the darkness, bouncing back louder and sharper than when it left my mouth.

Someone coughs. It isn't me. I spin around but the sensation is disorienting. "Sam?" My brother's voice quivers in the darkness.

"Nico?" I call out. Am I imagining him? Without meaning to, I shift. In wolf form, my eyes are stronger, and a shape reveals itself to me. It's Nico. He's lying on the ground—if there is a ground here—clutching his stomach. I pad over to him and nuzzle his hand. He strokes my nose then my head.

"Are you really here?" he asks.

I shift back and crouch down beside him. "I'm here."

"How?" Nico groans and I take hold of his arm.

"Stay still," I tell him. "Don't move."

"How are you here?" Nico asks again, coughing at the end of the question. "I saved you." Tears fill his eyes. "I wanted to save you."

"You did," I tell him. "You tried. But your mother... she pushed me in."

Nico sucks in a sharp breath, and I can't tell whether it's because he's shocked or in pain. Blood is seeping through the fabric of his clothes, making his fingers slick and red. "I'm sorry." He grabs my hand and squeezes it, leaving my palm bloodied too. "I'm so sorry." His speech is staccato'd now, and his face deathly pale.

"It's going to be alright," I tell him, pulling off my shirt and starting to rip the fabric into strips. "We just need to stop the bleeding."

Nico doesn't reply. His eyes roll back, and his body goes limp, but he's still breathing; I can see his chest moving slowly up and down.

Quickly, but not quickly enough, I tie several strips of fabric together. I lift Nico's shirt gently, exposing a deep wound in the center of his torso—right above his belly button. "Tanner can fix you," I say gently, scrunching up a ball of fabric and pressing it to the wound.

The pressure makes Nico cry out. He turns his head

sharply to the side and groans loudly, but I grab his hands. "Press this here." I push his palms down on the ball of fabric. "Press while I position the bandage."

Nico does as I say while I stretch my makeshift bandage over the tops of his hands. When it's in place, I tell him he can stop. "Okay, now hold the bandage while I lift you up."

With a breathy groan, Nico shakily holds the bandage in place. I hook my arms under his and pull until he's sitting up, then lean him into my chest, take hold of the bandage, and yank it tight around his middle.

He cries out as I fasten it, but I pull as tight as I can, squeezing the ball of fabric against the knife wound. When the bandage is fixed, I tear off several more strips from my shirt and repeat the process. This time, all Nico has to do is hang limp in my arms. When I'm done, I ease him back to the ground. Already, the bandages are damp with his blood. I might have slowed his death, but I haven't prevented it. Not yet. And I won't unless I can get us out of here.

I'm kneeling on the ground next to Nico, trying to slow the frantic thoughts in my head, when the blackness around us slowly turns into something else. Shadows appear. I can make out the shape of The Hollow, the wood, and the fountain. But they are empty. No one is there.

I stand up and turn around. Like I'm looking through a thick, grey gauze, I see it all. It's there, but I can't touch it or move through it. "Where are we?" I ask, lifting my arms and watching the thick air swirl around them like liquid smoke. "What is this place?"

Nico's eyes flutter open. He takes in our surroundings, then he says, "I think we're in hell."

3

LUTHER

We're at the treeline when Kole grabs Nova by the waist and throws her onto Snow's back. Without hesitating, Snow charges into the forest and disappears into the darkness.

Kole and I stop and turn around. We're in the shadow of the trees but Tanner is just outside. He's staring at the swarm of flies heading in our direction. I lunge for him and tug his arm, but he won't budge. His arms are rigid at his sides. I step in front of him and shake his shoulders. "Tan, we gotta go, dude."

His eyes are black. He starts to tremble.

"Kole, help me," I yell.

As Kole tries to force Tanner to move, I turn around and send a ball of fire from my palm into the encroaching swarm of flies. They dissipate for a second then reform, coming for us as if they're one being. Some kind of monster made of a million parts.

The noise is deafening. It makes my skin crawl and my brain itch. I try again. Another ball of fire, same thing. I cast a wall of flame like Nova's, but it's smaller. Too small, and the swarm simply rises above it. I have no idea what will happen if it reaches us, but I sure as hell don't want to find out.

"It's no use. Grab him." I gesture for Kole to take hold of Tanner.

In one swift movement, Kole heaves our friend onto his broad shoulder and runs. I follow behind, sending explosions to slow down whatever the fuck it is that's chasing us.

We're still running on the dirt track that leads into town when I realize the noise has stopped. My feet and my heartbeat are thundering so loudly that I barely notice its absence at first. At the same time, Kole and I slow down. He lowers Tanner to his feet.

"They're gone," he says, panting heavily.

I lean onto my knees and suck in a deep breath. My lungs are tight, my skin still itching.

"I can still feel it." Tanner's voice is barely a whisper. The color has drained from his face. Even his hair, usually a dusky blond, looks darker. He meets Kole's eyes. Something flashes between them as Tanner repeats, "I can still feel it, Kole."

Kole glances at me. "We need to get back to the cabin."

"Can you walk?" I ask Tanner.

He doesn't answer. He's shaking his head, muttering something under his breath.

"Tanner, can you walk?" I repeat.

Still silent, he nods and starts to move but he's painfully slow.

Eventually, we reach the outskirts of town—the road that merges with Main Street and runs right past the bar. We should skirt around and avoid coming into contact with anyone, but with Tanner the way he is it'll take even longer.

As if he's reading my thoughts, Kole tells me to wait with Tanner. "I'll find transport. Wait here."

He jogs off down the road and disappears around the

corner. I turn to Tanner and gesture for him to sit down. Silently, he lowers himself to the ground and brings his knees up to his chest. Wrapping his arms around his legs, he shakes his head.

"What happened back there?" I ask, crouching beside him.

Tanner blinks at me. He swallows hard and rubs the back of his neck. "Whatever came out of her mouth," he says quietly. "It was evil." He meets my eyes. His are soft at the corners, swimming with emotion. "Pure evil. I've never felt anything like it." Tanner taps his head with his index finger. "It was in here. I felt it growing inside me. I can still feel it."

A shudder trips down my spine. None of what just happened makes any sense. Nico was stabbed in the guts. Sam fell into a giant hole. Eve coughed up a swarm of evil black flies, and Ragnor rose his corpse bride from the dead.

Talk about a mind-fuck.

But while I'm reeling from it, trying to figure out what it means and what the hell we're supposed to do next, Tanner *feels* it. He feels all of it. Fear, grief, maleficence... evil.

"What about at the fountain? Were you going to do what I think you were going to do?" I ask. I've never heard the gritty details of what Tanner did for the League when they held him prisoner, but I know it was dark, and—back at The Hollow—I sensed something in him I've never felt before. A darkness I thought only lived in myself.

"Yes," Tanner says. "I was."

"Why didn't you?"

There's a long pause, then Tanner says, "I wanted to. My head wouldn't let me."

I put my hand on his shoulder. "Probably a good thing, Tan."

He grimaces a little and looks down at his hands. Then, looking up at me, he says, "The voice. You heard it?"

I nod solemnly. "You think it was...?"

"It was him." Tanner is scratching his arm now, digging his fingernails into his flesh. I grab his hand to stop him, and he meets my eyes. In barely a whisper, he says, "It was The Shadow King."

I suck in a deep breath. Before I can reply, the sound of a large diesel engine makes us both look up. An old white truck rounds the corner, coughing out fumes and littering the air with its noise.

"Get in," Kole rumbles through the rolled-down window on the passenger side.

"Who's is this?" I ask, climbing inside and watching Tanner slide in next to me.

"Found it outside The Cross," Kole says. "Keys were on the dash."

"Didn't Pete the vamp drive a truck like this?" Tanner asks, pulling the door shut.

"Yep." Kole does a U-turn and heads back in the direction he came from. "But I'd say he owes me, wouldn't you?" He fixes his eyes on the road and I nod in agreement; Pete sold Kole out to the League then took over his bar. So, yeah, he fucking owes him.

As we drive down Main Street, it strikes me how eerily quiet everywhere is. The manic energy that seemed to grip the town a few short hours ago has faded. There are no lights and no signs of movement. "Where is everyone?" I ask, frowning as we pass Rev's place—even her lights are off.

"Maybe they felt it," Tanner replies. "Maybe they felt what is happening."

"What *is* happening?" I ask. "I mean, what happens now? Did we stop it? That voice—if it is The King—has Nova's name. But they didn't take her. So, does that mean something went wrong? Or was all this just about Ragnor getting his dead wife back? And the *real* shit's going to happen later?"

Kole doesn't answer me, and neither does Tanner. My

litany of questions simply hangs in the air between us, making the air tight and clammy. Usually, I'd keep those kinds of thoughts to myself. Make a list. Investigate. But right now I need to know I'm not the only one feeling like we just fucked something up.

For the next few minutes, we sit in silence. When we reach the turn-out at the edge of the wood, we park up and head for the cabin. Signs of Snow's thundering footsteps are everywhere. Crushed leaves, broken twigs, bent saplings.

As we approach, I rub my palm over my closely shaved hair and clench my jaw. Kole is striding out ahead of Tanner and me; the blood bond he shares with Nova is pulling him toward her at speed.

At the bottom of the steps, I stop and take hold of Tanner's elbow. "You remember when I built this place?"

Tanner blinks at me as if he's surprised by the question. "It was half-done by the time I arrived," he says.

"Yeah, but you and Kole helped me finish it." I meet his eyes. "It was like therapy for all three of us. It gave us something we needed... time to heal."

"What's your point, Luther?" Tanner asks, pushing his fingers through his hair.

"Nova hasn't had time to heal from what Johnny did to her, or what happened to her parents, or what Thessaly showed us at the commune, and now she's lost her brother."

Tanner clearly thought I was about to start lecturing him because defensiveness is etched all over his face. But right now, I'm more concerned with Nova than I am with the effects of his jumping.

I meet his eyes. "She hasn't had time to heal from any of those things, and she's not going to get the time. Not yet." I fold my arms and sigh. "What I'm trying to say is that I'm guessing what happened back there is just the beginning, which means Nova needs us to be strong for her. You're the expert on emotions, Tanner. You know her better than any of us. You know what's inside her. You've felt it since the day you met her."

Tanner shakes his head. "I—"

"You have to stay strong for her." I reach out and squeeze his shoulder. "I know you can do it, Tanner."

He's about to reply when we hear Nova scream.

4

NOVA

I have no idea how long it takes to get back to the cabin. Snow is soft and warm, but when he stops—huffing loudly into the dark night air—I realize the fur around his neck is damp from my tears.

He stoops toward the ground, and I slide off him. My chest is cold without the heat of his body against it, although I'm surprised I can feel the cold at all. Usually, when I flame like that, I'm running so hot that I'm immune to any warmth that isn't my own.

Suddenly, though, I'm shivering. Snow is still breathing heavily, but he walks toward me and nuzzles into my chest. I stroke his head and he makes a low grumbling sound that's almost like a purr. I expect him to shift back into Mack, but he doesn't. He moves around me and walks up the steps. At the door, he waits for me to open it then enters first, barely fitting through the doorframe, sniffing the air like he's checking for intruders.

He grunts at me, then turns and walks back through the door. When it closes, I move to the window and catch the white echo of his silhouette moving past the trees. He stops, as if he's straining his ears, then carries on moving.

I watch him until he's out of sight. Barely a minute later, he reappears, and I realize he's pacing the perimeter of the cabin. Patrolling until the others return.

I turn away from the window and slowly cross the living room. Alone in the dark, I stand stock still. Emptiness presses down on me as memories dance through the room like ghosts. I look at the stairs which lead to the bedroom. As if he's really there, I see Sam slowly ascending them, pausing to tap on the door, then pushing it open. I see his eyes widen and picture him watching me on the bed with Tanner between my thighs and Mack behind me. I see his face when he kissed me for the first time. I remember looking into his eyes and *knowing* he was the missing piece I'd been looking for all my life.

"I love you..." His words fill my ears and bring me to my knees. I wrap my arms around myself and fight for breath as guttural sobs pummel my body from the inside out.

I don't remember feeling this much pain the first time I lost him. I don't remember it hurting this much when my parents died, but perhaps it did. Perhaps it was exactly like this, and I've spent twenty years blocking it out because to remember would be too much.

Behind me, something moves. I don't stand up or turn around. It could be The Shadow King himself, come to extinguish me, but I don't care. He can take me. It would be better if he *did* take me; at least I wouldn't have to live through this pain.

A hand touches my shoulder. I turn and through eyes clouded with tears, I see Mack. He doesn't speak, just strokes my hair from my face and kisses my forehead.

His tenderness sends a lightning rod of anguish directly

to my chest. I want him to comfort me. I want him to take the hurt away and make it so I don't feel this way anymore because it's already been too long to bear. But at the same time, I don't want him to do that. I want to feel this—all of it—because how else will I know that Sam was real? That he was mine? That I really did love him, and he really did love me?

"It's okay, Nova." Mack pulls me toward him. He's naked, as he always is after a shift, and kneeling on the floor behind me. I lean into him and run my hands over his chest, peppered with hair but still smooth. I rest my head above his heart, but when it beats in my ears I jolt back. I push him away from me.

"It's not okay." I shake my head. I push him again. The push turns to a shove, which turns to me thumping him with my fists. "It's *not* okay. It will never *be* okay again."

I'm not hitting him hard, but the last shove I give him causes him to topple backward. I haven't hurt him, but the fact I'm taking my pain out on him makes me cry even harder.

I clutch my hair. Raw, acrid tears burn my throat. "Mack..." I say his name as if I'm calling to him from a distance. "Mack, he's gone."

Mack rights himself onto his knees and pulls a blanket from the couch, covering himself with it. "Yes, Nova," he says, keeping some distance between us, not attempting to touch me, "Sam is gone."

A scream escapes my lips before I can stop it. I stand up, whirl around, and swipe the collection of empty glasses and mugs from the coffee table. They shatter as they meet the hardwood floor. Fire blooms in my palms, and I hurl it at the couch.

I scream again. Mack calls my name, but I don't hear him.

Flames surround me. I'm going to burn this place down. The whole fucking place. If I can't be here with Sam, I don't want it here at all. I don't want to be here. I'll set it alight and let the flames have me.

A silhouette moves toward me through the fire. Not Mack; there's no way he could. It's Luther. As if my heat doesn't touch him, he slams his hands onto my arms and squeezes hard. "Nova, stop." He meets my eyes. "Stop."

"I can't," I shout. Then in a whisper, I say it again. "I can't."

"Yes, you can." He pulls me to him and envelops me in his arms. Fire swirls around us, but then a wave of water washes over us. It takes my breath away. Instantly, the flames die. Spluttering, I stagger backward.

Luther lets go of me. He's drenched, and so am I. Tanner is over by the sink. He's incredibly pale, bracing himself on the countertop. The tap is dripping. Water soaks the floor. Kole thumps the tap to stop the incessant drip-drip-drip.

The four of them watch me but don't speak. I start to shake. My entire body is trembling. Then the room goes black.

* * *

WHEN I WAKE, I'm upstairs in the bedroom. It's still dark outside. For a moment, one glorious moment—just a fraction of a second—a smile twitches my lips. The bed is soft and familiar and warm. I am safe here. Here in the place where I've felt the most loved I have ever felt in my life.

Then I remember.

I see it all over again; Sam's face, Sam falling, Sam being swallowed by the Earth.

"Here." Luther helps me sit up and presses a glass of whiskey into my hands.

I drink it down it one drink. It burns my throat and makes me cough.

"Okay, now another." Luther tops the glass up with a bottle he took from next to the bed and watches as I wrap my hands around it.

My head is swimming. "It really happened, didn't it?" I say quietly.

"Yes, it did." Luther rubs his palm over the top of his head. Things have been different between us ever since Thessaly showed us her vision of The Original Six, yet I'm still surprised it's Luther who's here.

As if he feels like he should apologize for being the one at my side, Luther says, "Kole and Mack are reinforcing the shield."

"And Tanner?" I ask.

"Tanner's finding it tough," Luther says. "There's a lot of emotion in the air right now, and he's still reeling from whatever the fuck came out of Eve's mouth back there."

"The flies," I mutter. "I thought maybe I imagined it."

"'Fraid not." Luther moves a little closer and rests his hand on my ankle. His thumb rubs small delicate circles on my skin as he continues. "At least, we think they were flies. Tanner said they were *evil*. They chased us but stopped when we got to the edge of the wood outside The Hollow. They left Tanner pretty shaken up. The whole thing did."

My brain can't make sense of what Luther's saying, but he doesn't seem to understand it either. I take a sip of whiskey. I can barely taste it, but it's warm on my throat. "Ragnor?" I ask, barely able to speak his name.

"Last I saw, he was running back inside The Hollow with his zombie wife."

"Sam's mother," I say quickly, my eyes flashing with heat.

"Yes." Luther softens a little. "Sam's mother."

There's a long pause while I stare down into my drink. "What do we do now?" I ask when I look up.

"Now?" Luther slides up next to me and hesitantly wraps his arm around my shoulders. "Now," he says, "I think we have to prepare ourselves, Little Star. Because I have a horrible feeling that was just the beginning."

5

SAM

As Nico speaks, the air around us starts to shake. A figure appears in the distance, silhouetted against the dark haze of the forest. Watching my eyes widen, Nico says, "Sam? What is it?"

I look from him to the figure. "You don't see that?" I ask. "Someone is out there."

Nico's eyes flutter open, then closed; he's struggling to stay awake. "I don't... see..."

Panic grips my chest. Nico is dying. I need to get him out of here. I need to get us *both* out of here. Back to Nova, and the cabin, and the others. Back *home*.

I look up at the sky, praying for a sign—any sign—that Nova's world is up there somewhere, but there is nothing. Just thick gray cloud and an eerie white moon. I turn back to the figure. It's walking toward us. As it approaches, I realize it's a man. Under six-feet tall but thick-set with large bulky shoulders and clenched fists.

Something about his frame is familiar. A shudder runs down my spine. The scars on my torso feel suddenly hot and tight. "Frank?" His name stings like acid on my tongue. "It can't be. He can't be here."

Fear strikes my chest, grips it tight, squeezes my ribs until they feel like they might snap from the pressure. I crouch down and grab Nico's shoulders. "We have to get out of here." I try to move him, but he is too heavy and groans as I pull him. "Nico, help me, we have to go, we have to hide."

My voice is different; quieter and younger. I remember when I used to sound this way—when I was a child, then a teenager. When I was scared. Always scared.

Frank is drawing closer. His feet stomp the ground and make it shake. He seems taller now, like a giant against the landscape of The Hollow. I'm starting to shake. I heave Nico hard and this time I manage to start dragging him through the dark gray mist toward the fountain. I pull him behind it and hold my breath. Then suddenly, we're not outside The Hollow anymore and we're not hiding behind the fountain.

We're in a dark, dank basement hiding beneath the stairs. Frank's shadow falls over us. I stare up at him. He steps into the light that's shining down in a narrow beam from the door at the top of the steps. I take in every inch of his snarling face. It is just the way I remember it; full and slightly swollen with red cheeks and a scar that makes his top lip curl.

He flexes his fingers at his sides. I open my mouth to speak but nothing comes out. I scoot backward but my back hits the wall. Next to me, Nico isn't moving. I curl my body over his as Frank's heavy boots take a step closer.

"You've disappointed me again, Sam." Frank puts his hands on his hips. His stomach is large. It flops over his waistband and strains against the buttons of his plaid shirt. Slowly, he rolls up his sleeves then he moves his hands to his belt.

"I'm sorry," I whisper. "Please don't hurt us. I'll do better next time. I swear."

"There will be no next time." Frank whips his belt free and curls it around his hand. Then he comes for me. The blows rain down on my head, my neck, my shoulders, my back. He is indiscriminate. Usually, he tries to keep the marks hidden but tonight he doesn't care, and this fills me with dread. He's going to kill me. I know it in every fiber of my being; tonight is the night he will finally kill me.

When he stops, my entire body vibrates with pain. Beneath me, Nico hasn't moved. He is still breathing, but he's not awake and I'm glad he can't see me.

Blood drips down my face. I think my ear is bleeding. I raise a hand to it and flinch. Everything hurts.

Casually, like he's getting dressed after a long hot shower, Frank puts his belt back on then smacks his palms together and lets out a long heavy sigh. "This is the last time you'll see me, Sam," he says. "In two hours, a man will come for you. He'll take you away, and you'll never darken my door again."

"Take me where?" Although I hate it here, terror grips my stomach. "What will he do to me?"

"That's his concern, not mine." Frank sniffs loudly and straightens his sleeves. "Goodbye, Sam."

He turns and walks into the darkness of the basement. I watch his back until it disappears. I look at my arms, but the deep red marks that decorated them a few moments ago have gone. My ear is no longer bleeding. My head is no longer throbbing.

I'm about to stand up when Frank's shadow falls over me. He flexes his fingers at his sides. I open my mouth to speak but nothing comes out. I scoot backward but I hit the wall. Next to me, Nico isn't moving. I curl my body over his as Frank's heavy boots take a step closer.

"You've disappointed me again, Sam." Frank puts his hands on his hips. And then it starts all over again.

6

MACK

"Sam's gone. Ragnor brought Elena back from the dead. Kayla's on the run, and Eve's—" I stop speaking when I hear footsteps on the stairs. Kole and I reinforced the shield and have spent the last ten minutes talking about what the fuck we're supposed to do next. I expected him to have answers, but it seems his insight has been used up.

"And Eve's even crazier than she was before?" Luther asks, raising an eyebrow as he pads down the steps ahead of Nova.

I nod slowly. "And more dangerous."

While Luther heads for the kitchen, Tanner rises to his feet and crosses the room, taking Nova's hand when she reaches the bottom step.

Even when she first arrived in Phoenix Falls, I never saw her as fragile. Yes, she had scars—both emotional ones and physical ones from that fucking asshole Johnny—but there was a strength inside her that shone from her eyes. Right now, that sparkle is gone. As if she's a ghost or something not quite here, she keeps hold of Tanner's hand and lets him guide her to the singed couch.

If Luther minds that she scorched the place he built with his bare hands, he isn't letting it show, which is unusual for him.

Kole brings her a mug of coffee. She takes it but doesn't look at him. It will be daylight soon, and I'm not sure if that means it's too late for coffee or if time has stopped meaning anything at all since last night.

Luther tells her she should eat and starts rummaging in the fridge, but Nova doesn't reply.

Sitting down on the coffee table, I put my hands on Nova's knees. She's colder than usual and clearly exhausted. "I'm sorry," I tell her. "I'm sorry about Sam, Nova."

I want to tell her I understand the pain of losing a sibling. For the first time in a long time, I want to open myself up. Expose my deepest darkest memories so she knows I truly *know* how she is feeling.

But this isn't about me; it's about her. And talking to her about Layla right now won't do anything to ease her pain.

For a long moment, Nova doesn't meet my eyes. When she finally does look up, she blinks back tears then she turns to Kole. He's lingering by the window, arms folded, a blanket of misery quivering around him. As if he knows what she's about to say, his jaw twitches and he widens his stance—bracing himself for what's to come.

"You knew, didn't you?" Nova asks quietly.

I breathe in slowly and glance at Tanner. I think we were all hoping Nova wouldn't put the pieces together and realize that Kole allowed Sam to leave the cabin *knowing* what would happen if he did. But she's smart, and she notices things, and there's no way she wouldn't figure it out.

Tanner presses his lips together. He's barely spoken to Kole since we got back and is having a hard time remaining neutral. Clearly, he's also pissed that the seer in our group didn't warn us about what was going to go down.

Kole fixes his eyes on Nova's. "Yes, Little Star, I knew."

As if she expected him to lie, Nova frowns. She stands up and walks over to him. When she's close, she looks up and—for a second—I think she's going to collapse into his chest and let him hold her while she cries. Instead, smoke begins to dance on her skin. "Fuck you!" she yells. "Fuck you for lying to me!" She punches his chest far harder than she punched me. While it doesn't physically hurt him, it's obvious Kole is wounded in other ways. "You told me you loved me," she says, arms quivering as she stands back and meets his eyes.

"I do love you." Kole's reply is steady and sincere.

"If you loved me, you wouldn't have let my brother die." Nova's eyes widen as the words leave her mouth, as if she knows she shouldn't be saying them but can't stop herself.

Kole breathes in slowly, then he reaches out and brushes the side of her face with his index finger. Without saying another word, he turns and walks out of the door.

Nova watches him leave. When the door swings closed, she starts to cry again. As Tanner jogs after Kole, Luther and I move in unison toward Nova. When we reach her, her body folds in on itself and she sinks to the ground. We move with her. She's shaking from head to toe, and I can't bear to see her breaking like this.

Inside my head, Snow lets out a pained growl. He can't stand it either.

I pull her into my lap and wrap my arms around her. She leans into my chest, crying against my neck. Her tears start to soak into my shirt but then Luther takes her hand. He tugs her arm. "Stand up," he says.

Nova curls away from him, pressing harder against me. "Luther," I warn him.

"Stand up," he repeats, hooking his arms under hers and heaving her to her feet.

Shaking, she turns her face away from him.

"Luther, leave her." I stand up, too, and position myself behind her.

Ignoring me, Luther opens his palm. A flame appears. He flexes his fingers, and it grows. Nova's eyes are captivated by the flame. Like a moth that can't turn away, she stares at it and its warmth licks her face.

"Take her clothes off." Luther looks over Nova's head at me, meeting my eyes. For a moment, as I realize what he's going to do, I think about refusing. But honestly, I have no idea how else we can ease her pain. So, I do as he says.

7

NOVA

Mack is behind me. A toxic mixture of rage and grief sweeps through my veins, leaving me trembling and my eyes struggling to focus. I am *so* angry with Kole but overriding the part of me that longs to be close to him takes so much strength I can barely breathe. I might not be able to break the blood bond between us, but I can drown it out. It's hard, but I can do it.

"Take her clothes off." Luther is talking to Mack. Despite myself, a muted hum of anticipation trickles through my veins. Maybe this is what I need; maybe this is the only way to survive the pain I'm feeling. Maybe if I let them take it all away, I stand a chance of getting through it.

Mack hesitates, then does as Luther instructed. He hooks his fingers under the hem of my shirt, and I raise my arms as he lifts it over my head. Dropping it to the floor, he unfastens my jeans next. Luther watches as Mack tugs them over my hips, then he crouches down and removes my shoes. One at a time, he lifts my legs and eases my pants over my feet. When he stands, he skims his palms over my outer thighs and my hips. Then he waits for Mack to finish what he started.

"It's too bright in here," I whisper, looking at the lights above our heads. Right now, everything is too raw—too fragile—and the thought of being exposed in such brightness makes me shudder.

I expect Mack to reprimand me; to remind me that I'm his and if he wants to see me in the light then it's not my place to argue. But as if he *knows* that now isn't the time to push me to be strong, he leaves me standing in front of Luther and flicks the switch by the door.

We are plunged into darkness. It takes several seconds for my eyes to adjust. Only the smallest amount of moonlight makes it past the clouds outside, so we are now little more than silhouettes to one another.

When Mack returns to me, he unfastens my bra and slides the straps over my shoulders. My nipples stiffen as the cool night air caresses them. While Luther removes my panties, I allow myself to lean back into Mack's chest. He's shirtless but wearing the light gray sweatpants that I swear he must have a lifetime's supply of somewhere. I want warmth from him, but his skin feels cool on my back. He runs his hands down my sides, then loops his arms around my waist, holding me tight.

The pressure eases the knot of nauseating butterflies in my stomach. I close my eyes and squeeze his hands, encouraging him to tighten his grip on me.

When I'm completely naked, Luther stands up and leans in close. He sweeps a loose strand of hair from my face and, in the darkness, searches for my eyes. A flash of orange colors his irises. "Do you trust me, Nova?" he asks darkly.

I study his eyes. A few short days ago, I'd have said I wasn't sure. Now, I'd trust him with my life. "Yes," I reply quietly.

"Then close your eyes." He nods at me. I feel Mack stiffen a little, his muscles twitching.

I do as I'm told. At first, when I close my eyes, I see Sam's face. The sound of him calling my name echoes around the room. I flinch but Luther whispers, "Keep them closed."

As I screw my eyes shut tight, I notice something—a flicker of heat. But it's not coming from me. It's as if someone has lit a candle and is holding it close to my face.

"Do you feel that?" Luther asks.

I nod, keeping my eyes closed.

"What about this?" The heat moves down my body. It dances over my throat, then my chest. It caresses my collarbones, my shoulders, my arms. When it touches me, warmth pools on my skin and I exhale slowly. When it disappears, the cold that replaces it makes me wince.

Soon, it reaches my stomach. Then it becomes two flickers of warmth instead of one. They move over my hips and down my legs, then travel up to the inside of my thighs. Instinctively, I widen my stance and allow the heat to cradle my core. I sigh and reach up to hook my arms around Mack's neck. As I do, his hands cup my breasts. He licks his thumbs and slowly moves them over my nipples.

I turn my face and bury it in his neck. It's not right for me to lose myself in them. It's not right for them to take away my pain; I should feel it. *All* of it.

The warmth leaves my core. I whimper, but then it's there again. This time, higher up, traveling over my torso toward the space between my breasts.

Mack takes his thumbs from my nipples and, instead, cups my face and leans down to kiss me. As his lips meet mine, a short sharp *burning* sensation shocks my left nipple. Like I'm being scalded, a flash of pain makes my eyes fly open. I look down to see a flickering yellow flame in Luther's palm. He meets my eyes, the fire dancing between us. Then, holding my gaze, he brings the heat closer.

For the second time, he moves it close enough to my nipple to make me yelp. I search his face, my eyes wide.

"It won't burn you," he murmurs, flicking a flame into his other hand and moving both toward me at the same time. "A fire witch cannot be burned by a magick flame."

Somehow, knowing that the heat can *hurt* but not *burn* makes me release a long slow breath. Arching my back a little, I push my breasts toward Luther. "Do it again," I tell him.

So, he does… he brings the heat to my nipples and lets the fire lick at them. Pain and pleasure bleed together and send a rush of arousal through my veins. When Luther takes the flames away, I am left panting, my legs shaking.

Mack's hands are caressing my hips and I can feel his cock growing hard against my ass. "Shit," he breathes. "I've never…"

"You never played with fire before, Baloo?" Luther asks him.

Mack doesn't reply, just moves to my front and takes both of my hands in his. "Sit down, Little Star," he tells me, "and spread your legs for me."

I do as he says, not caring how my stomach looks from this angle or whether it will be uncomfortable for him on the floor. I wait for the warmth of his tongue, then grind into it as he begins to lap and suck my clit.

Tilting my head back, I look up at Luther. I reach for him and unfasten his jeans, pulling them roughly down over his hips. As his erection springs free, the piercings on his shaft catch the light of the dancing orange flames that now hover in the air between us. I take him deep into my mouth, as far as he'll go, and flick my tongue over the metal. Luther presses his palm against the back of my head and holds me in place, groaning with pleasure as my lips work his cock.

While he fucks my mouth, and Mack works expertly on

my clit, Luther sends his fire to explore my body. Licking my skin, it lights up every inch, every muscle, every sinew. Sometimes, the heat is gentle and soothing. Sometimes, it makes me cry out—like boiling water is splashing my flesh.

Luther takes his cock from my mouth and leans down to kiss me, then he nudges Mack out of the way and takes his place between my legs.

Shit. He's going to use the flames on my pussy. Holy hell.

My body stiffens in anticipation as I wait for the heat to collide with my clit. There is a quivering moment of cold, and then it's there. Dancing, pulsing, teasing.

I realize Mack is lying down on the floor beside us. Almost instantly, Luther lifts me up and positions me over Mack's cock. As I slide onto him and he fills me up, Mack groans and grips my hips. Even though I have my back to him, and he can see nothing but my ass, he stiffens inside me.

I wriggle into position, causing another groan to fly from his mouth, then lean back a little so Luther can return to my clit as I grind onto Mack's cock.

"Careful down there, Luther," Mack breathes. "Air mages *can* be burned by magick fire."

With a deep chuckle, Luther begins to toy with my clit. At first, without the fire, but then it's back. As the first spear of pain rocks my body, an orgasm rolls toward me. It's approaching fast, and I'm bracing myself for its impact when Luther stops. The warmth disappears. The pain fades and with it my orgasm does too.

I whimper and look down at him. "Don't stop. Why did you stop?"

Luther simply shakes his head at me, then starts again. This time, when I'm about to come, I slam down harder onto Mack's shaft, hoping the impact will send me over the edge.

But when Luther stops playing with my clit, and replaces the heat with cold harsh air, I growl with frustration.

As I lurch forward and grab Luther's face, bringing him up to kiss me, Mack's fingernails sink into my hips. He jerks up into me and growls, "I'm going to come, Little Star." But then he lifts me off him and whispers, "Not yet. I'm not done yet."

In a smooth almost-as-if-they-rehearsed-it movement, Mack and Luther switch places. Sitting up, Luther rests his back against the side of the couch and pulls me into his lap. I wrap my legs around him and gasp as he fills me up, still surprised by the feel of his pierced shaft inside me. Flicking my hair back from my neck, Luther peppers my throat with kisses.

"The fire," I groan. "I want the fire."

Without hesitating, Luther's flames are back. They skim my body like red hot pebbles on a smooth lake. I lean back as he moves the flames to my nipples, but my cries are muffled by the feel of Mack's impressive erection on my lips.

I take Mack hungrily into my mouth as Luther reaches between our writhing bodies and strums my clit. With one hand at my core, and the other still tormenting my breasts with his flame, he changes the angle of his hips beneath me and I lean back, bracing my hands on his strong, thick thighs.

This time, as my orgasm builds, I try to control my breathing, try to keep it steady and my face from becoming flushed because maybe if Luther doesn't know it's coming he won't try to stop it.

Despite my efforts, though, he knows. "Do you think she's ready?" Luther is speaking to Mack, who reluctantly looks away from the sight of my mouth devouring his shaft to say, "Has she earned it?"

Luther takes the heat from my nipples, then lowers his head to sweep his warm wet mouth over them. Heat, cold, wetness. Heat, cold, wetness. And the whole time, he doesn't stop making torturous circles around my clit.

"Please," I beg, letting Mack's cock slide out of my mouth and kissing Luther hard on the lips. "Please let me come."

Luther searches my face for a moment, then nods. With a determined groan, the circles quicken, bringing swirls of ecstasy to my cunt. My clit is warm, then hot, then *too* hot but he doesn't stop. I cry out as pain lights up my body. Sparks fly from my skin. From Luther's other hand, fire licks my breasts.

Next to me, Mack is moving his fist up and down his throbbing erection. He is standing, but jerks forward and braces his hand on the arm of the couch as ropes of hot cum land on my chest.

Luther yells and wraps his arms around me. The pain subsides, and the heat fades, and then finally I come. My body stiffens, every molecule fizzing with heat and fire and pain and pleasure. Luther pulls me into his chest, not caring that Mack's cum is now staining his shirt. He holds me tight as he comes, filling me up until there's no more room.

As my body collapses into Luther's arms, Mack kisses my forehead. "Good girl," he whispers. "You're such a good girl."

His praise washes over me. I close my eyes, then feel Mack wrapping a blanket around my shoulders. He helps me up and pulls the blanket tight as I shiver. "Let's clean you up," he says, gesturing to the bathroom.

Luther is standing too. He takes my hand. In a daze, I follow them to the shower and let them position me under the hot stream of water. "Do you want us to stay?" Mack asks as steam swirls around his naked body.

I nod and reach out my hands, then I pull them under the water with me.

8

KOLE

For the first time in weeks, The Hunger twists my insides. I catch myself licking my teeth, and immediately slam my fist into the nearest tree. The force of the punch sends a vibration down my legs. I whisper an apology and press my palm flat against its rough bark. My knuckles are bleeding, but I just stare at them transfixed.

I feel Tanner behind me before I see him. When I turn, he takes in my now-clenched fist and reaches for it to take a look. "She's grieving. She doesn't mean it." He glances up at me. He's lying to make me feel better, but I let him. "Here, move into the light, I'll take a look."

Tanner nudges me in the direction of the jetty. Together, we walk to the end and sit in the moonlight. I sit cross-legged while he kneels in front of me. "Just a graze," he says, twitching his fingers and beckoning droplets of water from the lake to land on my scratches.

I watch the water wash away the blood, then nod and say, "Thanks."

There's silence for a moment while Tanner turns his face toward the lake and looks out across its dark, unmoving surface. "You did know, didn't you?" he asks without looking at me. "You knew Sam would die if he went to The Hollow last night."

I sigh and reach up to unfasten my hair from its black elastic tie. As it falls loose over my shoulders, the release of tension in my scalp eases the stiffness in the back of my neck. "I knew," I reply slowly. "I saw it."

Tanner breathes in heavily through his nostrils. When I glance at him, they're flared and his eyes are dancing with something I haven't seen before—disappointment or disgust, I can't tell. "You let him go," he says quietly, his jaw tense.

"I had to." He knows this, but I say it anyway.

"Bullshit, Kole. You didn't *have* to. You could have..." Tanner trails off, rubbing his temples with his forefingers.

"Something happened to you back there," I say, moving so he has to look at me. "What happened?"

Tanner shakes his head as if he doesn't want to talk about it because he's still mad and wasn't done yelling at me.

With a frustrated sigh, The Hunger still gnawing at my stomach, I say, "Tanner, you know how it works. There are rules about what seers can share."

"Seems to me the rules can be bent when you want them to be." His eyes meet mine, and this time I know what's swimming beyond them—anger.

"It might seem that way, but that's not how it is." I stand up and brace my palm on the wooden post at the side of the jetty. "You think I wanted to do this to her?" I spin around at the same moment Tanner stands up. "You think I want to be out here, fighting the urge to drive into Red Rock and find the nearest F.H.B dealer? Instead of in there with Nova? You think I wanted her to look at me that way? As if she'll never trust me again?" My voice cracks and I turn back to the lake. I breathe slowly and heavily while every muscle in my body twitches with the need to go to her.

Tanner's hand presses lightly on my shoulder. He sighs and rubs my tattooed arm with his lithe fingers. "I'm sorry," he says quietly. "What happened back at The Hollow... it was a mind-fuck. We're all hurting." He moves his hand down my arm to grip my elbow, then steps in front of me. "I know you are too."

Of all the guys, Tanner is the only one I've shown any kind of weakness to over the years. But even he hasn't seen me truly broken. I saved my lowest moments for the times when I was alone.

Before I moved up to The Hollow, before I started to heal, I spent almost every night after the bar closed howling into the darkness of the apartment, hating myself for being so weak I couldn't fight the F.H.B. Hating myself for giving The Prophecy to the League because I was too weak to keep it from them. Hating myself for every minute I spent away from Phoenix Falls, for the years I spent floating from place to place, traveling almost the whole of Europe but with barely any memory of it because I was too high and fucked up to notice where I was.

Even *that* didn't feel as bad as *this*. A broken blood bond can kill a vamp. I'm not a vamp, but Nova and I *do* have the bond and, while it's not broken yet, it's strained to the point where it could quite easily snap.

I look past Tanner at the cabin. The lights are off, but a muted orange glow tells me they've lit a fire.

"She's okay," Tanner says, closing his eyes. "They're taking care of her." He frowns, wincing and shaking his head.

For the second time, I ask him, "Tanner, what happened to you back there? What's going on?"

Tanner pushes his fingers through his dark blond hair and bites the inside of his cheek. "I don't know," he says quietly. "I think it was just the force of it... of whatever the hell Eve sent after us. The strength of its darkness."

"What did it feel like?" I ask him as his face pales.

"Like death, and pain, and cold," he mutters. Then he inhales sharply and pushes back his shoulders as if he's trying to snap himself out of it. "I'll be okay." He rubs my arm again. It's an intimate gesture, not the kind we'd usually share, but I don't pull away. "I'll be okay," he repeats, looking up at me.

With my insides still tormented by the need to go to Nova, I hungrily pull Tanner's lips to mine. Our mouths smash together. He winds his fingers into my hair and pulls hard, moving his lips to my throat. I do the same, half-biting, half-kissing the side of his neck. My teeth are grazing his skin when he stiffens beneath me, and not in a good way.

"Kole," he mutters.

I don't want to stop. I want him to ease the ache inside me. I need him to do what he's always done—dampen The Hunger with his body, and his lips, and his cock.

"Kole," he mutters again, staggering back and holding me at arm's length. "I have an idea." He runs his index finger down his neck to the spot where my teeth left a small red shadow on his bronzed skin.

"I'm not going to bite you, Tanner," I growl. "That's not what I need from you."

"No," he says, "You're not. I'm the one who's going to do the biting."

9

NOVA

Early morning light hovers outside the window. Mack and Luther are sleeping. I'm supposed to be sleeping too, but even my third whiskey did little to ease the tightness in my chest.

The brief snatch of time I spent with Luther and Mack, letting them fill me up until there was no room for my grief, feels like a million years ago already. As soon as we stepped out of the shower, the relief dissipated and swirling, gnawing, anguish returned to my chest. They brought me to bed and curled themselves around me, clearly hoping that if they cradled me between them, exhaustion would take over and I'd manage to sleep for a while.

They fell asleep quickly. Their orgasms and the come down from the fight at The Hollow made their eyelids heavy and their breath slow. Now, they look peaceful. Both of them look so peaceful.

I lie still for a few more minutes before sliding out from between their arms and off the end of the bed.

The soles of my feet shiver as they meet the cold wooden floor. I'm wearing one of Luther's tees but move quietly to the chest of drawers in the corner of the room and take some of my own fresh clothes from it.

I wait until I'm downstairs to dress. Kole and Tanner are missing. I haven't seen them since I yelled at Kole, and the part of me that is bonded to him flutters with worry. Pushing the sensation away, I get dressed then take my sneakers from the shoe rack by the door. It's cold outside, quickly approaching fall, so I grab one of Mack's hoodies and toss it over the top of my own thin sweater. Then I snatch the keys to the truck Kole used to get the others back here.

On the veranda, I put on my sneakers and jog down the steps. I don't look back at the cabin, just head straight for the trees. At the turn-out just beyond the shield, I hop into the truck and start the engine. I'm a terrible driver but manage to turn the truck around and make it into Phoenix Falls with little trouble.

Town is eerily quiet. It's early, but there should be signs of life. People should be flitting about, opening the stores and cafes, heading off to work in other towns, walking their dogs, jogging on the trails by the river.

The entire journey, I see no one. By the time I reach Rev's, I'm starting to think the uprising has started already; Eve sent her deadly black flies to swarm through the town and kill all its residents.

Swallowing down a shudder, I park up at the back of Rev's then climb out and knock on the door. It takes at least a minute for her to answer. When she does, her eyes widen at the sight of me. "Nova? Holy stars, come in before someone sees you." She grabs my arm and tugs me inside.

In the darkness of the stairwell, she folds me into her arms. Tears fill my eyes and I try to fight them.

"What happened?" she asks, stepping back to meet my eyes.

As she frowns at me, I ask quietly, "Can we go upstairs? I need to speak to Sarah."

A flicker of understanding pinches Rev's face. She sucks in a heavy breath, and says, "Of course. This way."

I follow her upstairs into her small brightly decorated apartment. While I sit down at a small round table, she puts a kettle on the stove and leans back against the counter. "Do the boys know you're here?" she asks, tilting her head.

"No, they don't." I hug my arms around my middle. "I wanted to speak to Sarah alone."

Rev nods slowly, then moves into the center of the room and calls, "Sarah? Are you awake, honey? We have a visitor."

When Sarah appears, she looks like she hasn't slept in days. Her face is pale and gaunt, and she's holding her cardigan tightly around her small frame. "Nova?" A smile flickers on her lips, but then she looks around the room and realizes I'm alone. "You're here?" She frowns and moves closer.

I gesture to the chair opposite me. Slowly, Sarah takes it then leans onto her forearms and laces her fingers together. "Sarah, I need to tell you something," I say, looking down at my hands.

In the kitchen, the kettle is beginning to boil.

"It's about Sam." My voice cracks, so I clear my throat and close my eyes. I can hardly stand to look at her. "He's…" I force myself to meet Sarah's eyes. "Sam is gone."

Sarah blinks at me, then she glances at Rev, then back at me. Laughter bubbles in her chest. She shakes her head and laughs again. "Gone where? Where has he gone?"

"Ragnor was going to sacrifice Sam in order to bring back Elena," I speak the words that I rehearsed on the journey here. "He made a deal with The Shadow King; he'd find my name and hand me over. And in return, The King would bring Elena back for him."

Rev lets out a whoosh of breath and mutters, "Fuck."

Sarah simply stares at me.

"Ragnor's witch Eve performed some kind of ritual. The sky opened up, and a voice—The Shadow King's voice—told Ragnor he had to sacrifice his own blood in exchange for Elena's. He was going to kill Sam, but Nico jumped in front of him. Ragnor stabbed Nico instead."

"Nico?" Sarah is frowning at me. "Nico Varlac? The one who *pretended* to be Sam?"

I nod and press my palm flat onto the table. "Nico is..." My stomach twists, and I correct myself. "Nico *was* Sam's half-brother. Kayla and Ragnor's son. He tried to save Sam. He jumped in front of him, and Ragnor stabbed Nico instead."

Rev moves toward us and sits down in the third chair. "Holy hell, Nova."

"The earth was opening up like an enormous hole was swallowing everything. Nico disappeared, but I thought Sam was going to make it," I say, my voice on the verge of cracking. "Then Kayla..." I shake my head, "she pushed him. Sam fell into the hole. He tried to hold on, but he couldn't. Then it closed up, and he was gone."

Sarah slams her hand over her mouth and lets out a muffled cry.

"Sam and Nico are both gone." I look from Rev to Sarah. I expect tears to come again, to wrack my body and make me fold in on myself but this time they don't. Perhaps I have no more left.

"We felt it," Rev says quietly. "We felt something change in the air last night. The entire town grew cold." She meets my eyes then stands and walks to the window that looks down onto the street. "It was like evil arrived, and we could all sense it. The bars closed. Everyone went home, and this morning?" She gestures to the window. "There's no one around. It's as if everyone is hiding but has no idea what they're hiding from."

I rub my thighs and try to remember the moments before Snow took me away. "Eve—Ragnor's witch—conjured a swarm of flies from her mouth. The flies chased Luther, Kole, and Tanner then stopped on the edge of the woods."

"And The Shadow King?" Rev's voice catches in her throat. She presses her lips together and folds her arms. "Did he rise?"

"I don't think so. I think it was just the beginning. I think this was all about Ragnor and Elena—"

"Gone where?" Sarah cuts off my question, reaching for my hand and grasping it with hers. "You said Sam is gone, but where has he gone? He can't have just disappeared. He wasn't hurt. You said Ragnor stabbed Nico, not Sam. So, Sam must be *somewhere*." Sarah is squeezing my hand so hard that my fingers are turning white with the pressure. "We just have to find a way to get him back." She meets my eyes, nodding at me. "Right? We have to find a way to get Sam back?"

"Sarah," Rev says darkly, "if Sam's in The Shadow King's domain, there is no way to get him back."

Standing up quickly, Sarah shakes her head at us. "I don't believe that," she says. "There has to be a way." She pulls her sleeves down over her hands and starts worrying the cuffs with her fingers. "I'd *know* if he was dead. All the years he was missing, I knew he was alive. I felt it." She strides into the center of the room. "I feel the same way now. Sam is still out there." She waves her finger at us like a schoolteacher telling off a pair of unruly pupils. "I'm not giving up on him." And then she spins around and disappears back into her bedroom, leaving Rev and I alone.

"Do you really think...?" I trail off. Something dangerously close to hope is flickering in my belly. "Do you really think Sam could be alive?" I stand up slowly and brace my hands on the table. "Rev? Is it possible? Could he be out there somewhere? Waiting for me to find him?"

Rev closes her eyes and takes a deep, slow breath. When she opens them again, she says, "Nova, it's *possible* but—"

A smile flickers on my lips. That's all I needed to hear. "If he's out there," I tell her, "I'll find him. No matter what it takes, I *will* find him."

10

KOLE

The sun is creeping up over the horizon. We've been talking for at least two hours, but I'm still almost shaking with anger. "How can you even consider it?" I grunt, pacing back and forth on the jetty with the sun at my back.

"Tanner..." This time, my tone softens as he looks at me. "You've jumped twice in the past few weeks. Both times, it fucked with your head. Last night, you came into contact with maybe a tenth of The Shadow King's power and it's left you—" I wave my arms at him. "Damaged."

"I am not damaged," he snaps back through gritted teeth. "I'm recalibrating. I'll be fine."

I roll my eyes at him. "Even if you are... what you're talking about is completely different. It's another level. It's dangerous."

Rising up to his full height, he fixes his gaze on me. "Look me in the eyes," he says, "and tell me she's not worth it. Tell me you wouldn't do anything in your power to stop her from hurting the way she is right now. Tell me you wouldn't do anything in your power to give her Sam back."

My ears are throbbing. The sensation of my blood thickening in my veins is almost impossible to ignore. There are too many things in my head. The way I want Nova, the blood bond, the urge to get high, the urge to use Nova to get high, the thought of Tanner sinking his teeth into her pale skin. I let out a guttural roar and kick the post at the end of the jetty. It doesn't budge and leaves my toes throbbing. This time, Tanner doesn't come to my aid; he's already stalking back to the cabin.

"Tanner," I call after him. "Where the fuck are you going?"

"I'm going to talk to the others," he yells back. "We vote. As a group. Like we always have."

I'm about to run and catch him up when I stop myself. Am I scared for Tanner or Nova? Am I scared Tanner's plan won't work? Or that it will?

I'm at the steps, about to take them two at a time and convince the others this is a terrible idea, when the door clatters open. "She's gone." Mack strides out onto the veranda. In a flash, he's Snow and he's sniffing the air. He barrels past me before I can ask what's happened.

Luther appears next, looking half awake and worried as hell. "She's gone." He repeats what Mack said. "We woke up and she was gone." He's about to run after Snow when I catch his arm. "Papa Bear will find her. We need to talk."

Frowning at me, Luther gestures to the trees. "Kole, she could be in trouble—"

I shake my head. "She'll be fine."

"Something else you know but can't tell us?" Tanner's voice drifts toward me from the doorway of the cabin. He's leaning against the doorframe.

"I don't know where she is," I tell him. "I just know she's okay. She's not in danger. I'd feel it."

Tanner rolls his eyes at me and disappears back inside.

"What's going on?" Luther folds his arms and narrows his eyes at me.

"Tanner's pissed because I knew what would happen to Sam and I didn't stop it." I bite the inside of my cheek almost daring Luther to be pissed at me too.

He simply nods. "Right."

"And he has a dumb-ass idea that's going to get him killed." I push past Luther, ready to let hell loose on Tanner.

He's on the couch, leaning his forearms onto his knees, and looks up when I walk in. "Have you *seen* me dying?" he asks, his eyes snapping to meet mine.

I stop dead in my tracks. Luther steps into the room behind me and watches us both as I try to find the words to answer Tanner's question. "No, I haven't seen you dying, Tanner."

"Have you seen *anything* to do with what we've been talking about?" Tanner raises his eyebrows. "Anything at all that tells you it will end badly?"

"No," I mutter. "I haven't."

"Have you seen anything that tells you Sam has to stay wherever the fuck he is in order to stop The Shadow King?"

"No," I say again. "I have not."

"And you're telling me the truth?" Tanner asks, tilting his head.

"Yes, I'm telling the truth."

"Well, then—like I said—this is something we decide together. We vote."

"Vote on what?" Luther finally speaks up, looking from me to Tanner because he has no idea what the fuck we're talking about.

Tanner stands up slowly. "We vote on whether I should use Nova's blood to magnify my powers and jump into hell." He flexes his fingers at his sides and stares at each of us in turn. "We vote on whether we try to bring Sam back."

11

SAM

The memory of Frank's basement replays and replays and replays until I can't take it anymore. I feel like I'm breaking. I can't breathe, can't think, can't move. When it fades, relief washes over me. But when I open my eyes, I'm on stage in *Spine*. And this memory is almost as bad as the last.

As my wolf brothers eviscerate my skin with their teeth, I beg my mind to take me somewhere else. I know now what's happening; I'm being tortured. Visions of my past are going to torment me until I lose my mind. There is no escape. Even though I *know* what's happening, I can't stop the fear and the pain from overwhelming me. The wounds are as raw as they were the first time, and there is no way to soften them.

As the memory resets itself and I'm once again standing in the spotlight waiting for my brothers to pounce, I look at Nico.

He still isn't speaking or moving. He's with me, even though he is not part of this memory. I have no idea if he's seeing what I am or if his mind has taken him to a torment of his own. His breath is shallow in his chest. Perhaps he's reliving the moment his father plunged a knife into his stomach, or perhaps his punishment is that he will remain like this—*dying,* not dead—forever.

When the wolves attack, I don't feel the way I did the night Nova found me. I feel the way I did the very first time it happened; terrified. Convinced I'm going to die. Teeth rip open my shoulder. They are perilously close to my neck. Madame's voice rings out. "Enough! He must live!" Blood soaks my skin.

I screw my eyes closed. Any second now, it will start all over again. Stage. Spotlight. Music. Teeth. Blood. Pain.

Except this time daggers of white light force me to shield my eyes. When the light fades, we're no longer in *Spine,* or Frank's basement, or on the lawn at The Hollow. Around us, turrets of black rock reach up toward a dark red sky. Clouds move swiftly across it as if time is moving at three times its normal speed.

The ground is black too but covered in deep grooves that glow orange in the dim light.

The same gray gauze that half-obscured The Hollow hangs around us. Still half-naked, I shiver as I move through the gray. The mist clings to my skin and makes it prickle. In front of me, a section of black rock drips with something that could be blood. Half-congealed, it tumbles slowly down toward the ground where it pools and spreads.

Movement coming from behind my back makes me stop. I feel a dark shadow looming over me. I turn slowly, fear twisting my insides. I'm afraid to look but at the same time, I know I *have* to look.

When I do, I fall to my knees.

A *creature*—because that is the only possible way I can describe him—cocks its head at me. Its eyes flash with the same bright light that made me shield my eyes only, this time, I can't move. My arms are pinned to my sides. Even my fingertips are frozen.

It is standing. Like a man, it has two legs, but they are not the legs of a person; they're twisted like gnarly tree trunks and bowed in a way that should make it impossible for the thing to move. A scrap of dark cloth hangs around its middle, but its chest is bare. At its sides, it flexes two sets of long, clawed fingers.

"You are not supposed to be here," it says.

Instantly, I recognize its voice. It is the voice from the sky; the one that spoke to Eve and Ragnor.

"The Shadow King," I whisper.

The creature ticks its head to the side for a second time. It has a man's head, but no distinguishable features. A flat nose, thin lips, eyes which are so sunken they almost don't exist. Dark gray skin stretches over its cheekbones, pulled taut and almost translucent. The same skin covers its entire body. I can see its heart beating, black inky blood pulsing through its veins. It is both there and not there at the same time. If it wanted to, it could walk right through me.

"I have many names," it says, moving its gaze to Nico.

"Is this...?" I look around as thunder rumbles through the dark red sky. "Hell?"

The creature snaps its eyes back to mine, then opens its mouth and laughs. Its laughter merges with the thunder and grows louder, shaking the rocks and the ground. When it stops, it says, "This place has many names too." It takes a step closer and reaches out, dragging a long, pointed fingernail over my bare chest.

I swallow hard. It's difficult to breathe. I feel as if someone is squeezing my chest, wringing my lungs free of oxygen. The Shadow King studies me for a moment then flings out his arms. As he does, lightning slices through the sky. There's another clap of thunder and a vibration that I feel deep in my soul, then the rocks start to crumble. They fall, disintegrating into tiny fragments, melting as they drop into the pool of molten blood. I drop to the floor and grab hold of Nico. Then the noise suddenly stops. The rocks and the sky become some kind of hall. Grand, with a flagstone floor, and dim flickering lamps on the walls. The Shadow King stalks away from me then sits down on what looks like a large black throne. Ebony feathers decorate its back. Skulls form columns on either side of it.

The King places his hands on his twisted thighs and inhales deeply. "Bring me the hounds," he says loudly.

I remain crouched on the ground, clasping Nico's hand. There's the sound of a door—large, metal, heavy—being opened. Then a noise that is so familiar it brings tears to my eyes; the baying of wolves. I look quickly from one side of the hall to the other. Large pillars conceal the edges of the room. Only dark shadows are visible, and it is almost impossible to tell which direction the sound is coming from.

Soon, I realize it is impossible because the sound is coming from *all* directions.

Flashing yellow eyes appear in the darkness. I hear the gnashing of teeth. Growls fill the air. Instinctively, I shift. As a wolf, I at least have a *chance* of protecting my brother. I stand in front of Nico, snarling. The hackles on my back are raised, and I lower my head ready to pounce.

But what appears from the darkness is not wolves or dogs or anything I recognize.

They are shaped like wolves, and they sound like wolves, but they are *not* wolves. They are something far, far worse.

A whimper escapes my mouth. I find myself pressing my belly flat to the floor, cowering beside Nico as the beasts approach.

From either side of the hall, they creep into the light. Like The King, they are covered in thin gray skin that allows their bones to protrude at strange angles. They have ears, but they're pressed flat against their skulls. They have teeth, but their jaws are far larger than any wolf I've encountered.

One of them lifts its head and bays at the ceiling. Another joins in. The Shadow King closes his eyes and tilts his head back as if he's listening to heavenly music.

Soon, at least twenty of the wolf-beasts are sitting in front of the throne. I shift back and stagger to my feet so I can see over their heads.

"We have her scent," The King booms. "We have her name."

The beasts howl and yap and bark.

"Find The Phoenix and bring her to The Hollow," he calls as a quivering image appears in the air beside him.

"Nova," I breathe.

The King's eyes flash white as he watches the image. Nova is being carried by Snow. She's on his back, and they're running through the forest. Then she's inside the cabin. The others are there too, and they're all staring at her as she screams. She starts a fire. Tanner puts it out. She looks broken. Utterly broken.

I shake my head. "No," I mutter, "no, you can't."

But the sound of the King's beasts drowns out my voice. Saliva drips from their open mouths as they howl at the ceiling. The image changes, shimmering and shifting until it shows The Hollow instead of the cabin. There are no signs of the devastation that took place. The ground is normal, and Eve's altar is gone. All I can see is the fountain but then Eve appears. She trots down the steps, staring straight ahead.

Can she see us? She moves quickly until she's so close it's like she's on the other side of an open window. She blinks her black-rimmed eyes and raises a hand. She's holding a dagger; the same one Ragnor used to make Nico bleed.

Lifting her palm, she slices a large deep gash into it then

lowers her head and laps at the blood. When she looks up, her lips are stained red. She smiles, then she thrusts her hand forward. It appears above us, larger than it should be, shimmering and not quite there.

Eve's blood begins to drip from her palm. It splashes onto the floor.

How is she doing this? How is this happening?

"Come, my darling," she calls. "Set the hellhounds free. Send them to me. Send them to Earth and let them devour her."

My blood runs cold.

"Send them to me and let them turn The Phoenix to ash." Eve twists her hand so her blood flows more freely. The Shadow King snaps his fingers and, instantly, the hounds rush forward. They lap at the floor, drinking Eve's blood. They turn their mouths to the ceiling and catch the drops falling from her outstretched hand. Then as she takes back her hand, they jump.

One by one, they leave the hall and jump through whatever the fuck that hole is until there are none left. They are all with Eve, scraping the earth outside The Hollow with their large, clawed feet.

Eve stands in front of them, waving her arms as if she's conducting a choir. Then she looks back at the creature sitting on the throne. "Soon, my King. Soon, you will join us too."

Slowly, The Shadow King rises from his throne. "Remember to capture her blood," he growls. "Without it, I cannot cross over."

Lowering her head, Eve closes her eyes. "You have my solemn promise, my King."

"Good. Then let it be done."

In a split second, the portal is gone. Eve is gone. The Hollow is gone. I yell and lurch forward. "Nova!" I scream as if somehow, some way, she might be able to hear me. "Nova!"

The Shadow King returns to his throne.

"Nova!" I drop to my knees, and he watches me as I call for her. I shout until my voice is hoarse and my chest is wracked with pain. All the while, he watches. Then finally he starts to smile.

"Don't worry, Sam," he says. "She'll be here soon."

12

NOVA

Rev is pouring hot water from the kettle into two large mugs. The drink she gives me smells of cinnamon and lavender. "Are you trying to put me to sleep?" I ask, taking a long sip.

"I'm trying to calm your nerves," Rev says, "and mine." She moves from the kitchen to the couch and sits down, tucking her legs up underneath her.

I join her in the living room but take the large navy-blue armchair by the window. I pull a blanket around my shoulders and wrap my hands around the mug.

"The boys will worry when they realize you're missing," she says, watching me over the top of her drink.

"I know."

"You should call them." She reaches for her phone and offers it to me. "Want to use mine?"

I shake my head. "Maybe in a little while. For now, I just need some quiet."

Rev nods slowly. She sips her drink without speaking.

"Kole knew," I say quietly.

"He knew?" Rev fiddles with one of her large, hooped

earrings. Her hair is pixie short and adorned with a brightly colored scarf. Despite it being early in the morning, she is ridiculously glamorous.

"He knew what would happen to Sam. He saw it in a vision, but he didn't stop it."

Rev closes her eyes for a moment. When she opens them, she says, "It is the way with seers. There are rules we simply can't break. Especially seers from traditional families like Kole's."

"Can't or won't?" I reply quickly.

Rev tilts her head from side to side. "A little of both."

"I hate him for it." As I speak, my stomach twists violently.

"No, you don't," Rev says.

"No," I reply. "I don't. But I wish I did." I glance over to Sarah's door, then tuck my feet up onto the chair beneath me. "What do you think she's doing in there? Should I go see if she's okay?"

Rev shakes her head. "She knows we're here. If she wants us, she'll come out."

I'm taking another sip of tea, wrinkling my nose at the strange sensation of drinking lavender, when a thunderous banging on the door downstairs makes us both leap to our feet.

Tea sloshes onto my hand, but I barely feel it even though the skin pinks beneath the droplets.

"Wait here." Rev puts down her tea and hurries to the door. She closes it behind her, and I hear her footsteps trot quickly down into the stairwell. Then I hear, "Mack? What the—"

I remain seated, my heart quickening in my chest as heavier footsteps approach. The door swings open, and the sight it exposes would almost be funny under different circumstances.

Butt naked, Mack stands in the doorway with his hands on his hips. I scan his body appreciatively and laugh despite the ache that now lives rent-free in my chest. "Morning, Professor." I raise my eyebrows at him.

"You disappeared," he says, striding over to me.

It's hard to keep my eyes on his face, but when he crouches in front of me and I see worry etched into the corners of his deep brown eyes, I set my mug down on the windowsill and cup his face. "I'm sorry if I scared you."

Pressing his lips to mine, Mack steals a hungry kiss. He sweeps my hair from my neck and kisses the spot just below my ear. "Don't run away again, Nova. Please. Not now. It's too dangerous."

I'm staring into his eyes when the sound of Rev clearing her throat makes me look up. Eyebrows twitching, she gestures to Mack's butt, waving her hand at him as if she should be shielding her eyes. "Not a flattering angle, Mack," she says, looking away.

Without even a glimmer of embarrassment, Mack stands up. I'm about to pass him the blanket from my shoulders when Rev shakes her head.

"Oh no," she says. "That was my mother's blanket. It's not going anywhere near your man parts. Wait there."

As she disappears back downstairs, Mack perches on the edge of the chair. I'm used to his nakedness by now, but it still surprises me how at ease he is with being completely exposed. I rest a hand on his thigh, allowing myself to enjoy the sensation of his warm skin and wiry leg hair beneath my palm—not too hairy, just the right amount.

"Are you alright?" he asks, lacing his fingers with mine.

"I'm fine," I tell him, trying to smile. "I just had to see Sarah. I had to tell her what happened."

Mack nods slowly. Stroking my chin, he tips my head up and kisses me again. When he stops, he presses his forehead to mine and says, "What Luther did with the flames...it's dangerous, Nova. He can control his fire. He knew what he was doing, but—"

"You're worried I'll let someone who doesn't know what they're doing torture me with fire?" I tilt my head and frown at him. "The five of you are the only ones I'd ever—" I stop, aware of how ridiculous it would have sounded just a few weeks ago if I'd heard myself saying I was exclusive to *five* guys, not just one.

Mack blinks at me. I wonder if he's about to correct me—tell me there's no longer five of them because Sam is gone—but he doesn't. "Actually," he says softly, "I was worried you'd try playing with Luther and end up burning something delicate."

"*Nothing* about Luther is delicate," I quip.

For a long stretching moment, everything feels remarkably normal. Mack is deliciously naked, we're making fun of Luther, and he's leaning in to kiss me. Then out of nowhere, my chest tightens. I rub it with my palm and close my eyes, willing the sensation to subside.

"It'll take time," Mack says gently. "A long time. Some moments, you'll forget. You'll feel normal. Then you'll hate yourself for feeling normal." He slips his arm around me and I stand up, allowing him to move into the chair and slide me onto his lap. "Just don't shut everyone out like I did. I can't afford to wait thirty years for you to open yourself up again."

I stroke his beard with my index finger. I'm about to loop my arms around his neck and nuzzle into him when Rev appears in the doorway and snaps, "Rhone Mackenzie, get your naked ass out of my favorite armchair."

Chuckling, Mack stands up and catches the clothes Rev tosses to him. "Lucky for you, I started stocking men's wear a while back."

Mack holds up a pair of skinny black jeans and a

matching black t-shirt. "These are more Kole's style than mine," he says, but stops talking when Rev hurls a black pair of boxers and a teal sweater at him too.

"Stop complaining and for the moon's sake get dressed." Rev is trying not to laugh.

As Mack moves toward what I assume is the bathroom, he wiggles his eyebrows at me. "She's only asking me to get dressed because she's worried she won't be able to control herself around my god-like form much longer."

I giggle and pull the blanket up closer to my chin. It still feels wrong to laugh, but the sparkle of hope—the one that ignited in my belly when Rev told me it was possible for Sam to still be alive—is easing the conflict.

"I'll make you some tea," Rev calls, placing the kettle back on the stove. Then to me, she says, "He knows what you're going through. He can help you. If you let him."

I breathe in deeply. "Perhaps I won't need to." I meet her eyes across the room. "If we bring Sam back, I won't need to *go through* anything."

Rev opens her mouth to reply, then changes her mind. Without saying anything, she turns back to the kettle and watches it until it boils.

13

MACK

It took some fucking effort to appear cheerful just now. Snow is pacing inside my head like a maniac. He can't stand seeing Nova hurting, and the half hour it took us to run here from the cabin was like torture for him. He lost Layla. He can't lose Nova too. Neither can I.

"It's okay, buddy, she's safe," I mutter to myself.

It's not lost on me—the weirdness of my symbiotic existence with Snow. It's hard to put into words, but even harder to imagine what it would be like without him in my head. We are one being, and two beings at the same time. He is me. I am him. We are each other.

And yeah, I know that makes me sound like a fucking transcript on an ancient scroll or something Kole ordained from the skies. But it is what it is.

The pants Rev gave me are horrendously tight-fitting. I'm used to gray sweatpants after a shift, and fashionable slacks when I'm dressed properly. Not jeans that make it impossible to move and cut off my circulation.

The shirt isn't much better. When I emerge from the bathroom, though, Nova looks approvingly at me. "Suits you," she says, standing up and crossing the room to slot her hand in mine. "You should wear black more often."

Still uncomfortable, I pull the teal sweater over the black t-shirt, then sit down at the table. Rev hands me a mug of tea I just *know* is going to taste disgusting. It smells like bath salts or a grandmother's perfume.

"Just drink it," she says disdainfully.

After one sip, I put the mug down and glance toward the living room. "Where's Sarah?" I ask. "Did you speak to her?"

Nova sits opposite me. "Yes," she says quietly. "She doesn't believe Sam is dead."

I notice the lilt in Nova's voice. Instantly, my stomach clenches. Rev is watching us from the corner of the room; she noticed it too. "Nova," I say firmly, "we saw him fall."

But Nova simply shakes her head. "We didn't, actually," she says, her eyelashes fluttering as she meets my gaze. "We saw him holding on, then he lost his grip, and the ground closed up. We didn't see him fall and, even if he did, we don't know what he fell into. We don't know *where* he fell into."

I glance at Rev. She shrugs her shoulders and grimaces a little as if she's already had this conversation with Nova and isn't sure what else she can add.

I breathe in slowly, feeling my nostrils flare. A long silence stretches between us. I tap my fingers on the table then say, "Nova, Sam was taken to…" I trail off and look at Rev. She nods at me but doesn't come to my aid.

Nova has folded her arms and is staring at me. "The underworld?" she says. "Hell? A dark place full of demons and devils and—" She scoffs a little, and I feel Snow's growl rumbling in my chest.

"Yes," I say darkly. "That is precisely where he was taken."

"But it *is* a place," she says. "A real place. Not an intangible fairy-tale kind of place like *Heaven*. A real place."

I search her face, then try to summon the part of me that

used to be good at explaining this kind of thing. I take her hand across the table and stroke her palm with my index finger. "Nova, as supers, we grow up learning about the constructs that hold our universe together. We are taught about the existence of different dimensions. We take classes on demons and devils and learn spells to ward them off. We learn about the three comings of the underworld—times in Earth's long history when The Shadow King succeeded in breaking through but was eventually locked back into his own dimension by brave and powerful mages."

Nova swallows hard. "He has succeeded before?" she asks quietly.

"Three times," I tell her. "The last was over ten *thousand* years ago."

"Ten thousand?" Nova asks, her voice barely a whisper.

I nod solemnly. "He has remained in the darkest of our dimensions—the one we now call the underworld, but which humans call Hell—for ten thousand years. Waiting to return."

"Why didn't you tell me this before?" Nova asks, searching my face.

"I'm sorry," I tell her. "I wish we'd had time. I wish I could teach you everything you need to know, but things are moving faster than we ever thought they would."

As Rev joins us at the table, she lights a candle and places it in our midst.

"We always thought there would be signs," I say, still holding Nova's hand. "We moved to Phoenix Falls because we thought there would be signs that the prophecy was going to be set in motion. But there was nothing—not a thing—until you arrived in town."

Nova looks at our hands, then takes hers back and puts it in her lap. "You're telling me Sam is in another dimension? The underworld. That's where he is?"

"I believe so, yes, but there's no way to know for certain."

"But that's what I said." Nova's eyes brighten. "He's not *dead*. He's out there somewhere."

"Nova, I don't think you're hearing me." My tone darkens. "No one has ever come back from a hell dimension. Especially not The Shadow King's."

"Yet," she says. "No one has come back *yet*."

Frustration bubbles in my throat. Either she's deliberately ignoring what I'm saying or she really doesn't understand. Perhaps she doesn't. Perhaps she can't; she didn't grow up with this. It's a foreign language to her. Too complex to learn in the few snatches of conversations we've been able to have these past weeks.

I'm about to try a different way of explaining when a loud wailing sound shatters the air.

"Sarah?" Rev springs to her feet and rushes to one of the doors that lead off the living room. Before she reaches it, the door springs open.

"I saw them." Sarah is shaking from head to toe. "I saw them." She's holding her wand, her fingers curled so tight around it that they're almost white with the pressure.

"Saw who?" Rev puts her hands on Sarah's arms.

Slowly, Sarah turns toward the window. She points a trembling finger. "Outside," she whispers. "They're outside."

As Sarah speaks, the hairs on the back of my neck begin to prickle. Inside my head, Snow releases a low warning growl. I stand and gesture for Rev and Nova to stay back, inching to the window. Pressing myself against the wall, I peer down into the street.

And then my blood runs cold.

"Mack?" Rev asks, moving tentatively forward.

"Stop," I hiss. "Nobody move." Down below, clawing at the sidewalk in broad daylight, a pack of hellhounds begins to howl.

14

NOVA

The color drains from Mack's face. He is pressed against the wall, frozen, not moving. Rev and I approach him slowly, instinctively flattening our bodies against the wall too. In the middle of the room, Sarah is still trembling except now she's also muttering and shaking her head.

A howling sound shakes the air. It makes Sarah slam her hands over her ears and sink to the floor, where she wraps her arms around her knees and starts to rock back and forth.

A trickle of ink-black dread drips down my spine. The noise fills my ears, my head, and my mind. But it's not wolves or dogs; it's something else.

"Mack?" Rev whispers.

When Mack turns to face us, his eyes are flashing amber. "They've come for Nova," he says.

Rev looks at me, but I can barely move. "What are they?" I ask, struggling to hear myself over the sound that is now swelling in the street, through the apartment, and every inch of Phoenix Falls.

"Hellhounds," Mack says, darting away from the window and grabbing my wrist. "We have to get out of here. Now."

Without another word, Mack tears across the room, dragging me with him. We hurtle down the stairs and he flings open the door. We are barely a foot into the street when something rounds the corner ahead of us.

A flash of teeth, surrounded by gray stretched skin, set with yellow eyes, and dripping saliva hurtles toward us. I can't count how many beasts there are; there isn't time.

Another hand takes hold of me. Rev is pulling us back inside.

She and Mack slam the door closed and lean on it as something barrels into the other side so hard that a large indent appears on its surface. Stepping back, Rev mutters a lock incantation. "It won't hold them long," she says, watching the door start to buckle under the pressure of the huge ravenous bodies that are slamming themselves into it.

"Upstairs. The roof." She grabs me and we take the stairs two at a time. When we reach the landing outside her apartment, she yells, "Sarah, stay inside. Bolt the door. Don't come out." Then she keeps running ahead of me all the way to the roof of the building.

When we reach the open air, I realize Mack isn't with us. My eyes widen. I'm about to lurch for the door and scream for him to hurry when he appears. "Tried a demon-repelling spell," he says, panting. "Didn't work."

"That's because they're not demons," Rev mutters, backing up toward the edge of the building.

"What are they?" I ask, pressing up against the cold brick wall and watching as Mack tries to reinforce the door to the stairwell.

"Hellhounds. Beasts. Not alive, but not dead. Legend says they're the only thing that can cross dimensions since The Shadow King's realm was sealed shut." Rev swallows hard and shakes her head, making her large earrings patter against her cheek. "I guess the legend was right."

"They want me?" I ask as Mack joins us, looking around as if he's hoping to find a parachute or a getaway helicopter.

"Ragnor gave The King your name. He wants you dead so he can rise." Mack's jaw twitches. "We knew he would come for you." He shakes his head and yells, "Damn it! We should have kept you safe."

"I ran away," I tell him. "It's not your fault."

"Who cares whose fault it is?" Rev says, eyes widening as she stares at the door to the stairwell. "What matters right now is how the hell we're going to get off this roof."

I look down over my shoulder. On the street below, I count ten baying hellhounds. Their jaws snap and their eyes flash as they stare up at me, willing me to jump or to fall into their waiting mouths.

Punching the screen of her cellphone, Rev lifts it to her ear, checks it's ringing them thrusts it at Mack. "Luther," he barks, "we need help. Hellhounds at Rev's. They've come for Nova."

I hear Luther say, "We're coming," then the line goes dead.

Mack nods at me. "It's okay. They're on their way."

But Rev replies, "Great, and what exactly will they do when they get here? 'Cause I sure as hell don't remember any lessons at the Academy on how to beat these things, do you?" She meets his eyes. "Seriously, Mack, do you? Do you know how to fight them?"

Mack shudders. His shoulders start to move. Undulating, stretching, snapping into strange angles. "I don't," he says, "but Snow might."

He ticks his head from side to side, lets out a deep vibrating roar, and then his clothes rip from his body as he turns into his other self. Seeing Snow's large, white frame towering above me, a momentary calm settles in my stomach. It'll be okay. Snow's here. It'll be okay.

Huffing, Snow stomps toward the door and plants his feet firmly on the ground. He looks at me and Rev, growls something at us, then turns back to stare at the door.

Looking around the rooftop, I grab Rev's hand. "We need to hide. Snow will fight them off, but we need to hide."

Rev points to a row of three large chimneys on our left. We run to them and crouch down. We have just managed to hide ourselves from view when the door gives way and the hounds stampede onto the roof.

Almost falling over one another, they fill the space between the door and Snow. They seem not to notice or care that a huge white bear is ready to take them on. They just come for him. They pounce, all at once, teeth and claws slashing at his fur.

Snow groans loudly and fights the first two off, shaking them to the ground and hitting them hard with the back of his paw. The third one lunges for his shoulder, but Snow's teeth sink into its neck, and he hurls it away. *He can do this. He can fight them*, I tell myself, still gripping Rev's hand in mine.

For perhaps an entire minute, Snow manages to stay in control of the battle. But then he releases a heartbreaking yowl and a deep red stain appears on his furry white shoulder. Another on his flank. Another on his side. There are too many of them, too many teeth and claws, and he can't fight them all. I try to move, but Rev keeps hold of my hand. I look at her and force a wave of heat into my palm.

Flinching, Rev drops my fingers. I stand up and pull my arm back, a ball of fire dancing in my grasp. I have exposed myself, but I don't care. The Shadow King took one of my mates, he will *not* take another.

Roaring at the top of my lungs, I hurl my fire bomb at the

hound on Snow's shoulder. It yelps and tumbles to the ground.

I send more. Another, and another, and another. When they're scattered on the floor, I turn the fireballs into a ring of flames, encircling Snow.

He drops to the ground and rolls onto his side, panting hard, blood soaking his fur in large ugly patches all over his body.

When the hounds rally, they turn away from the fire and position themselves in a line. They are snarling, staring at me, and gnashing their teeth when Rev pushes a rush of air in their direction. It is so strong that they are flung back into the wall opposite us. They yelp, but right themselves quickly.

"Your affinity is air?" I ask. "Like Mack?"

Rev nods, stretching out her arms and looking up at the sky. Dark storm clouds move quickly across it. The air around us begins to swirl. I pull fire into my palms again and stand stock still beside Rev. Confidence flickers in my gut. We can do this. We can fight them. I fought Eve. How much harder can it be to defeat a pack of wild dogs?

But even as the thought crosses my mind, it darkens.

The hounds are howling again. There is the sound of claws against concrete in the stairwell. I glance behind us into the street. "The others," I breathe. "They're coming."

As Rev pulls back her arms, ready to hurl a tornado at our attackers, I cast a protective wall of flames in front of us. The hounds stop howling. More appear from on the roof; there must be at least twenty of them now.

For a moment, they stare at us with their yellow eyes then one of them breaks ranks. It charges forward, straight through the fire, and doesn't even flinch as my heat singes its skin. It goes for Rev first and has its teeth around her wrist before she can stop it.

She screams as blood drips down her arm. When the

beast lets go, her hand is barely attached to her body anymore. She falls back, cradling her arm against her. She sinks to the ground, leaning against the wall. "Nova, run," she mutters. Then, louder, "Nova, RUN!"

I do as she says. I dart sideways, but the hound is at my heels. The others are in front of me, then they're all around me. They have me trapped. Heads down, heckles raised, they fix their eyes on me and lick their lips.

I am closing my eyes, summoning every ounce of fight left inside me when the sound of rushing water makes me look up.

A torrent of water sweeps across the roof, putting out my flames and knocking the beasts from their feet. It keeps going and smashes them into the wall opposite me, then I hear Rev yell. She is standing up, reaching out her uninjured hand, pushing the water with a blast of air until it lifts the hounds and throws them over the edge.

They squeal and yelp as they hit the ground.

Someone grabs my hand. I realize it's Kole. "Nova, hurry." He pulls me with him. "They won't stay down long."

"Snow and Rev." I turn and see Tanner wrapping an arm around Rev's waist and helping her to the door, but Luther isn't having the same success with Snow. He's crouched next to him, nudging him with an open palm.

"He won't wake up." Luther looks up at us. "I don't like his breathing."

Shaking Kole's hand from my arm, I sink to the ground and smooth my hands over Snow's bloodied shoulder. "Mack, you have to shift back," I whisper. "If you're in there, Professor, we need you back so we can carry you home."

Snow opens his eyes and turns his head slowly to meet my gaze. I stare into his dark brown eyes. They flicker with dots of amber. "Snow, send Mack back to us so we can help you." I stroke his face. He groans and leans into my touch.

Then he shudders, trembles, bends, and breaks until he is Mack again.

The sight of my beautiful professor's naked body covered in deep oozing wounds brings tears to my eyes. "Help him." I look up at Kole. "Carry him. Please."

As Luther helps heave Mack into Kole's arms, I move toward the stairs.

"Sarah." Rev's voice is croaky. "Don't forget Sarah."

"I'll get her." Tanner passes Rev to me, and I hook my arm around her waist. "The truck's out back. Go quickly."

He disappears down the stairs, and the rest of us move as fast as we can. While Kole climbs into the truck bed with Mack, Luther takes the driver's seat, and I help Rev in beside him. She is deathly pale and closes her eyes as she leans her head back.

"She's losing too much blood," I mutter.

Quickly, I pull off Mack's hoodie, then my thin white sweater. I rip it into strips and I'm about to try and wrap it around her hand when Tanner appears. "I'll do it," he says, climbing over me and turning his attention to Rev's hand. Then to Luther, he says, "Drive. Sarah's in back." At the same moment I pull the truck door shut, the howling starts again and Tanner yells, "Luther, drive. Now!"

15

LUTHER

I kick the truck into gear and drive. Fast. As we pull onto Main Street, the hounds spot us and hurtle in our direction. I look in the rear-view mirror and see Sarah sending sparks of something from her wand. Kole stretches out his arms and rips two large trees from their roots, sending them flying into the middle of the street, but the hounds just leap over them.

"Faster, Luther," Kole barks.

I press my foot on the accelerator, slamming it to the floor, but Pete the vamp's old beat-up truck is going as fast as it can. Next to me, Tanner is winding a bandage made from Nova's sweater around Rev's wrist. Her hand was damn near hanging off, and now she's conscious but not speaking.

Pressed up against the window, Nova looks in the side mirror and shouts, "They're not stopping." She turns to me and, over Tanner's head, says, "Can they break through the shield at the cabin? If we get there, can they break it?"

I glance at Tanner, and we exchange a look that says neither of us knows the answer. "I fucking hope not," I mutter.

As we round a corner up ahead and pull onto the road that leads out of Phoenix Falls, the sun hits the windshield in exactly the wrong spot. I'm blinded, for just a second, but I ease my foot on the gas and it's enough for the hounds to close the gap between us.

They're running either side of the truck now, bashing their unnaturally strong bodies into the doors.

"Shit." I struggle to keep the truck steady, then one jumps onto the hood. For an almost-comical moment, it holds its balance but then its legs buckle—like Bambi on ice—and one small jerk of the steering wheel sends it skidding off onto the road.

It tumbles into the trees, but there are at least ten more in its wake.

Winding down her window, Nova sends a spray of flames which engulfs the hound nearest to her. For a good few seconds, it seems unaffected but then she yells, turns up the heat, and it runs away with smoke coming off its gray skin. She does the same to the next, and the next, but she's getting tired.

In the back, Kole shouts as a hound jumps up beside him. It's about to pounce when a vine winds tightly around its throat and slams it to the ground. Sarah is cowering now, holding her wand shakily in front of her, aware her spells are of little use.

Kole takes down another hound, Nova does too, and then there are only two left. Sensing they can't get to Nova while she's protected by the truck, they slow up but keep following us.

"We're nearly there," I tell the others. "I'll park as close to the shield as I can. Nova, take Rev. Tanner, help Kole with the professor. I'll hold off the hounds until you're through the shield."

Nova mutters, "Luther, you can't. Not on your own." But I shake my head and tell her, "Don't argue, Supernova."

When we reach the edge of the wood, the truck's wheels spin on dry leaves as I slam on the brakes and park in the turn-out. Rev's eyes roll when Tanner tells her we need to get ready to run. After losing so much blood, the fact she's still conscious is a miracle.

In the back, Kole yells, "They're coming. Move fast!" The professor is *not* conscious. He's out cold and covered in deep ugly scratches.

Opening the door, Nova jumps out of the truck. Tanner does too and runs to help Kole heave Mack out of the back and carry him toward the shield. I help Rev down, then hand her over to Nova.

Sarah is still in the back. Nova shouts for her to hurry, and she snaps out of it, scrambling down and running toward the others. Ahead, six hellhounds round the corner. They stop in a line, scrape their feet on the ground, then run toward me.

As the others head for the shield, I create a line of flames in front of me—even though I know it won't stop them, I'm hoping it might slow them down but it doesn't, not even a little. They simply hurtle through it and head straight for me. I'm taking out one on my right when another leaps into the air. It's aiming for my throat. I'm bracing for impact when flames hit the side of its face. Instantly, its jaw catches fire. It howls and the flames spread over its face, down its spine to its tail.

When I turn around, Nova is standing behind me. Her eyes are different. They're wide and dark, and the fire in her hands is now bright white instead of flickering orange.

I'm about to tell her to run when she opens her mouth and screams. Lightning shoots from her fingers. The four remaining hounds in front of us stop, shaking while staring at her. Then as if it's nothing, she uses the lightning to lift the truck six feet into the air, hurl it towards them, and slam it down on top of them.

There is a cracking sound as their bodies break, then a whimper, then silence.

I study Nova's face. As I watch, the lightning fizzes away to nothing and her body droops with exhaustion. Her eyes are normal again, and I catch her as her legs buckle.

"What *was* that?" I ask, steadying her in my arms.

"I don't know." She shakes her head, staring at her fingers. "I just know I couldn't lose another one of you."

I smooth her hair from her face. It's damp and her forehead is clammy. I want to kiss her. Desire, lust, and love for how fucking incredible this woman is washing over me. But it's not safe. "We have to move," I tell her, wrapping my arm around her waist. "Come. Quickly."

* * *

When we reach the cabin, it's like a field hospital in a war zone. Rev is slumped in an armchair. Sarah is helping to hold her hand in the air, presumably to stop the blood flowing so freely, but her breathing is shallow and her eyes only flutter when we walk in.

Mack is on the couch, but Tanner is struggling to get a good look at him. "Clear the table," he says, standing up and waving at Kole. "Luther, help me lift him."

I take Mack's feet while Tanner takes his shoulders. Together, we manage to lift him onto the kitchen table. Tanner clicks a light into his palm and starts to examine the wound on Mack's shoulder. He's staring closely at it when Nova brings over a blanket and arranges it over the professor's middle, covering his modesty.

As Nova smooths Mack's hair, we all wait for Tanner to

say something. He straightens up, shaking his head, and extinguishes the light. "I've never seen wounds like this before," he says. "It's like they're infected already." He points to the raised, angry skin around the scratches then grabs his medical bag from the countertop. "I need to clean them," he mutters, almost to himself.

"I can do that," Nova says, moving to take Tanner's elbow. "Rev needs help too. Her hand…" She swallows hard. "If you tell me what to do for Mack, I can do it."

Tanner meets her eyes. "Alright, Little Star," he says, already taking small glass bottles from his bag. "Boil some water. Sprinkle this into it. Three teaspoons." He hands her a bottle full of what looks like light gray dust. "Then use cotton swabs to clean the wounds. When you're done, I'll take a look." He rummages again in his bag and takes out a bottle of pink pills. "Try to get him to take three of these. They'll help with the pain and the infection."

I follow Nova to the kitchen while Tanner starts on Rev's hand. Rev cries out as he removes the bandage, and I hear him curse under his breath. Kole stalks over to me and stands next to me while Nova returns to Mack and follows Tanner's instructions.

"We need to get out of here," Kole says darkly.

"Nova destroyed the hounds," I tell him. "She—" I frown, trying to put into words what exactly she did back there. "She moved the truck with lightning. Crushed them with it."

Kole chews his lower lip. "She's getting stronger," he mutters.

"I think it was fear," I tell him. "She thought they were going to kill me."

"We still need to leave." Kole unearths the whiskey bottle from below the sink and takes a long swig, then passes it to me.

"You think they'll make it through the shield?"

"I think he'll send more." Kole meets my eyes. "He'll keep sending them until they succeed. Now he knows her name. Now he knows she's the one, he won't stop until she's dead."

I don't know how much of what Kole's saying is summation and how much is from what he's seen about the future, but I'm not going to argue. "We can't leave until the professor's healed," I tell him.

Kole nods and takes back the whiskey. "Then let's hope that doesn't take too long."

16

NOVA

As I start to clean the deep, angry scratches on Mack's shoulders, his eyes open and he reaches for my hand. Relief washes over me. "There you are," I whisper. "You're okay, Rhone. We've got you."

He squeezes my fingers. "I like it when you call me that," he says.

"As much as you like it when I call you *Daddy?*" I ask playfully, trying desperately to make him smile so I know he's really okay.

Mack's lips twitch, but instead of smiling, he winces a little at my touch. "Never as much as that," he replies quietly, stroking my palm with his thumb.

"Tanner asked me to clean your wounds. You'll be okay." I pick up the cotton swab and the bowl and return to what I was doing.

Mack screws his eyes shut and mutters, "Fuck."

"Take these." Luther is holding out a glass of water and three of Tanner's small pink pills. Mack opens his mouth, and Luther presses the pills onto his tongue, then steadies his chin while he drinks from the glass. It's a tender gesture—the kind I wouldn't usually expect from Luther. But maybe I've underestimated just how much he loves his friends. Or as he calls them, his brothers.

Turning his head, Mack notices Tanner and Rev. "Is Rev alright?"

"She's okay. Tanner's working on her hand. It was in pretty bad shape." I pat his shoulder. "Stay still. This will take a while."

Mack looks back at the ceiling, clearly trying to focus on something other than the pain. Moving on from his shoulder, I turn my attention to the deep, nasty looking scratches on his chest.

"Is Snow alright?" I ask, unsure whether that's a silly question or not.

"He's resting," Mack says. "But he's very grateful to you for saving us."

"I didn't—"

"You reached him. You made him shift. If you hadn't, we'd have been stuck on that roof." Mack fixes his eyes on mine. "You saved us, Nova."

"Saved me too," Luther says, sitting down on the other side of Mack and starting to clean the cut on his wrist. He raises his eyebrows at me. "She lifted the truck clean into the air then dropped it on the hounds' heads."

I flinch at the memory. I still don't know where the lightning or the strength came from. "I wish I knew how to summon it," I say quietly. "On the roof, all I could do was create fire. I couldn't even make them explode."

"Couldn't Johnny them, you mean?" Luther says, concentrating on Mack's hand.

When he first coined the term, it made me feel a little icky. Like *Johnnying* someone shouldn't be something I was proud of. Now, it seems quite appropriate; reserved for the absolute worst kind of punishment.

"No. I tried on the roof, then when I saw them coming for you, but all I could manage was lightning." I turn to Mack because he's supposed to understand these things better than I do. "Why couldn't I do it? I tried to…" I paused, then give in and use Luther's nickname, "*Johnny* them but all that happened was lightning rods shooting from my fingertips."

Mack's fingers twitch as I slot my hand into his. "We've always known you have great strength, Nova. We just need to help you find a way to control it." He strokes my knuckles and adds, "You will find it. I promise. We'll help you." His lips twitch into a smile. "We just need to be some place safe for more than five minutes so we can have a few of those lessons I was supposed to give you."

"I know what your lessons likely entail," Luther quips sarcastically. "She needs *magick* tuition not 'how to be a good girl for your professor' tuition."

Surprisingly, a rumble of laughter shakes Mack's chest. "Fuck you, Luther," he chuckles.

"Fuck you too, Baloo." Their eyes meet and something passes between them. It looks like love—the love of two guys who have been brothers for so long they've forgotten how to live without one another. Luther squeezes Mack's good shoulder. Mack pats his hand. "Glad you're okay, man," Luther says quietly.

Mack nods. "Me too." He glances down at the blanket slung across his middle. "And glad someone thought to cover me up so I wasn't lying here like a cadaver in the middle of the living room."

"That was me," I tell him, taking hold of the corner of the blanket. "But now it's time to flip you over."

Luther helps me, easing Mack into a sitting position. He pats the table, encouraging Mack to lie down again—on his front this time—but Mack shakes his head. "I'm good like this," he says, shuffling the blanket across his lap again. "What little blood I have left is going to my head lying down."

By the time Luther and I finish cleaning Mack's back, the pills he took seem to be taking effect. The redness has subsided, and he's able to move more easily.

Over by the armchair, Tanner has been stitching Rev's hand and now smothers it in a thick pink cream; the same one he used on my injured hand after I smashed Kole's tattoo gun.

Rev is awake, and Sarah has brought her a cup of hot, sweet tea. She sips it, using her good hand to hold the mug.

"You might lose some function," Tanner says as he finishes winding a bandage around her hand then uses another strip to create a sling for it. "Or maybe some sensation in your fingers. This really should have been done in a hospital by a doctor." He pushes his fingers through his hair, biting his lower lip.

"You did a good job, Tanner," Rev says, smiling at him. "We both know we wouldn't have made it to the hospital if we'd tried to get there. I might have lost the hand altogether. Or my life." She meets his eyes and says, "Thank you. I mean it."

Tanner stands up. His hands are bloody, so he leaves Rev with Sarah and goes to wash up in the bathroom. While Luther and Kole help Mack over to the couch, I wait a moment, watching the bathroom door. When Tanner doesn't re-emerge, I follow him.

Without knocking, I push the door open and find him leaning on the sink, his large, beautiful shoulders shaking as he breathes heavily. When I touch him, he jumps. But when he realizes it's me, he pulls me to him with a force I barely recognize. Hungrily, he slams his lips onto mine and pushes my hair from my neck. Winding it around his fist, he tugs so that my head jerks back, then he plants a line of hot wet kisses down my throat.

"Tanner," I whisper. This wasn't what I came in here for. I followed him to make sure he was okay, to try and make him talk to me about what was going on inside his head. But when white hot arousal starts humming between my legs, and twists in the pit of my stomach, I forget all of that. I want him to devour me. I want him to fill me up and remind me that we're here, that we're alive, and that we have each other. "Fuck me," I tell him. "Fuck me so hard I see stars."

Tanner pauses for a split second, drinking me in, then he rips my shirt over my head and tosses it to the floor. He is moving quickly like he's never needed anything so much in his life. He doesn't take off my bra, just pulls it down and dips his head to bring his warm wet mouth to my nipples. Swirling his tongue over them, he unfastens my jeans. I reach for his too and fumble with the buttons.

His cock springs free, almost hard but not quite. I curl my fingers around it and feel him stiffen in my grip. Tanner catches my hand, then meets my eyes. "I need to be inside you, Nova." He searches my face. His expression is one of utter desperation. "I need to feel something good. I need to make you come."

Spinning around to face the sink, I remove my jeans and throw them to the side of the room. Tanner pulls my panties aside and settles his hands on my hips, nudging my ass out to meet his crotch.

I look up and see him in the mirror, staring down at my ass as he drags his hard, throbbing cock over my slit. "You're wet," he breathes, sending tingles through my entire body. "You're already wet," he says again, almost in disbelief.

I don't speak, just brace my arms on the sides of the sink, allowing my breasts to meet the cold, smooth porcelain. Tanner swipes a finger over my already-throbbing clit then without warning plunges inside me with such force I jerk forward.

I moan and tighten my grip on the sink. With one hand on my hip, and the other curled around me to toy with my pussy, Tanner fucks me. Hard. His chest glistens with sweat as we find a rhythm that makes us both moan and pant. He tugs my hair, pulls me onto him again and again, then holds me still and slams into me.

My cunt flutters as his length swells inside me. When he takes his fingers away from my pussy so he can grab my waist with both hands, I move my hand to my clit and make urgent circles. The orgasm that comes is quick and violent. I grab hold of the sink so hard I feel like it might shatter, shuddering as I jerk back onto Tanner's shaft. Tanner moves his hands to my shoulders and his fingernails dig into my smooth skin as he holds on tight and pounds into me. He cries out and fills me with his hot white liquid. We are both shaking when he lets go of my shoulders and kisses the spots where his nails marked me. Smoothing his hands over the expanse of my back, he kisses my neck, my ear, the groove between my throat, and my shoulder. I watch him in the mirror. He sweeps my hair to one side and kisses my neck again. His teeth graze my skin then there's pressure. A surprising amount of pressure. It makes me jump and he quickly takes his mouth away.

Standing up, he gathers our clothes. When I turn around, leaning back against the cold sink, he kisses my forehead. "Thank you," he says, pressing his forehead to mine. "I needed you so badly, Nova."

"I needed you too." I stroke the side of his face. But when I turn back to splash my cheeks with water, I catch my reflection in the mirror and notice the smallest shadow of a bite mark on my neck.

Since when was Tanner into biting?

17

NOVA

When we emerge from the bathroom, Sarah is making tea. She takes a tray over to the coffee table and hands each of the guys a mug. "What were those things?" she asks, finally seeming to have found her voice again.

Mack repeats a similar story to the one Rev told me on the roof; magickal beasts that are neither demons nor from the human realm. Beasts that are able to cross between dimensions because they belong in neither.

"They came for Nova?" Sarah says, glancing at me and pulling her sleeves down over her hands so she can fiddle with them. "Because she is The Phoenix?"

"Ragnor gave The Shadow King my name," I tell her in a matter-of-fact tone. We all know Ragnor only has my name because Sarah gave it to him and, although I know why she did it and have forgiven her, something inside me can't help wanting her to remember what she did.

"The King wants me dead because I'm supposed to stop the prophecy. Presumably, he's not able or willing to come to

Earth himself just yet." I look at the others for confirmation that they've come to the same conclusion I have.

Mack nods gravely. "I believe that's the case, yes," he says. "Otherwise, he would have appeared when Eve performed her ritual at The Hollow."

"Perhaps there is another ritual to be performed," Rev says. "Perhaps he simply doesn't want to risk coming into contact with Nova himself. She's supposed to stop him from rising, right? So, maybe he wants her dead before he attempts it. To make sure he succeeds."

Mack rubs his beard with his thumb and index finger. "It's certainly possible. He has been trapped in the underworld for thousands of years. However he intends to return to Earth, he needs Nova out of the way in order to do it."

"Why didn't Ragnor just kill her?" Tanner's question interrupts Mack's train of thought. As he looks around the group, I try not to allow myself to react to the fact they're all talking about me being *murdered* as if it's normal parlance now.

"Why didn't Ragnor kill her?" Tanner repeats himself. "He's had several opportunities. When he kidnapped Nova and Kole, and when we fled from The Hollow and came out here to the cabin. Nico said Ragnor and Eve knew where we were the entire time." He stands up from his seat on the arm of the couch and waves his arms at our surroundings. "They knew we were here, yet they waited to simply hand over Nova's *name*. Why?"

No one answers. Something flits across Kole's face. A few days ago, I trusted him more than I trusted myself. Now, every time I look at him, I wonder what he's keeping from me. Does he know something we don't? What else isn't he saying?

"We can discuss all of this," Luther says, pacing to the center of the room, "when we're somewhere safe."

Everyone looks at him.

"We can't stay here," he tells me as if I'm the one he has to convince. "We don't know what will come for you next, and we have no good vantage point here. We need to be somewhere more contained where we can spot what's coming and stand a chance of stopping it."

"A smaller area would be better," Kole says. "We can create a stronger shield if it's more concentrated."

"Where will we go?" I ask them. "Ragnor and Eve are still at The Hollow, and I don't think any of us are strong enough to try and throw them out. We can't go to Rev's apartment. I'm not putting her and Sarah in even more danger."

"We can if you need to," Rev says. "You know I'm in this with you, Nova. If you need to camp out at my place, it's yours."

"Thank you," I tell her, smiling and trying not to look at her bandaged hand.

"I don't think the apartment is the right place, Rev. We need you safe—and separate from us. The five of us need to figure out how to stop The King. But if we fail, we'll need someone in Phoenix Falls to raise the alarm. We also need you to be our eyes and ears in town. As far as we know, Nova's still wanted by the SDB. If agents return looking for her, we'll need you to alert us."

Rev presses her lips together and nods solemnly.

"*But*," Mack says, "Nova's right, we can't go back to The Hollow." Mack rubs his thigh with one hand and stares down into his tea. "We might never be able to go back there."

"What about the falls?" Tanner is standing by the window, looking out at the soft afternoon glow that has descended on the woods. He turns to face us and folds his arms. "There are caves behind them where we can set up camp, and caves above which will serve as a lookout point. Plus, there's magick there. We all know it. We've all felt it. Being close to them might—I don't know—help recharge us somehow. Or help Nova tap into her powers."

All three guys are nodding. "Can't think of a better suggestion," Luther says. "Kole? Mack?"

"I agree," Mack says. "We can stick to the woods to get there. It's the long way around, but if we loop around the town, we can reach the falls without risking being seen."

"What about us?" Sarah is sitting on a stool next to Rev. She worries with her sleeves constantly; it's making me nervous. "You're really going to leave us with no protection? Those beasts know Nova was with us. Doesn't that make us a target?"

"I don't think—" Kole starts to speak but Rev cuts him off.

"Like Mack said, they need eyes in town. If the hounds return, we'll fight them off." She grimaces and rubs her bandaged wrist. No one mentions the fact that, last time, we were all pretty much hopeless at fighting them off.

"And if something else comes for her?" Sarah asks, her eyes flashing with anger.

"We'll be okay," Rev says, putting her good hand on Sarah's shoulder. "Between the two of us, we can shield the apartment well enough to protect ourselves. As soon as they realize Nova's not here—whatever *they* are—they won't be interested in us anyway." She shuffles in her chair, sitting up a little straighter. "But we can at least buy Nova some time."

"Thank you," I mouth to her.

Rev nods. "Any time," she says quietly.

"That's settled then." Luther moves toward the kitchen. He glances at the clock on the wall. "If we leave in an hour, we'll be at the falls by sunset."

"Is Mack able to walk that far?" I turn to the professor. He's still pale, but the cuts on his arms seem to be healing.

"I'll be okay, Little Star," he says, nodding at me. "I'm

getting a little cabin fever stuck out here anyway. A change of scenery will be good."

"*Cabin* fever?" Luther retorts. "That's an old-man joke if ever I heard one."

"Well, he *is* an old man. What do you expect?" Tanner raises his eyebrows. For a moment, the air is lighter. Mack's eyes twinkle as the guys make fun of him, and the knot of anxiety in my chest eases a little. But then the moment is gone, and everyone starts moving, grabbing supplies from the kitchen, throwing things into bags.

"There's camping equipment in the attic," Luther says, raising his eyes to the ceiling. Kole offers to help him, and the two of them disappear. A few minutes later, several rolled up sleeping bags are thrown down the stairs along with the backpacks we took on our train journey to the commune.

I sit with Rev and watch as the guys pack up our lives. A lot has happened since we came out to the woods but, in a strange way, I've never felt as safe as I have in this place. "We laughed a lot here," I say to Tanner as he brings over a duffle full of my clothes. "I'm sad to leave it."

"We did a lot of other stuff here too," he replies, smiling cheekily at me.

"It feels like…" I trail off and rub my arms. "Like things are about to change. Like whatever's coming next is bigger, and scarier, and darker than anything that's happened to us so far."

Tanner breathes in sharply. I try to rein in the fear that's scratching at my insides because I know he must be feeling it. "I can take some of it from you," he says quietly, pressing his large palm to my chest. "Some of the pain, and the worry."

I shake my head. "No." I wrap my fingers around his. "You've got enough feelings of your own to deal with. You don't need mine too."

I'm about to ask him about the biting—to ask why he was tempted to do it and why he didn't go through with it—when Luther claps his hands and says, "Okay. We're done. Let's roll out, everyone."

18

KOLE

Leaving the cabin is necessary. We all know it and yet there is a resounding silence when we reach the bottom of the steps and look back. Rev and Sarah wave to us from the veranda. Rev's arm is in a sling but, thanks to Tanner's nursing, she's regained some of the color in her cheeks. She and Sarah have agreed to wait here overnight, then return to town in the morning.

"Did you ever explain to the hospital why you went AWOL?" I ask Tanner as we turn away and begin our slow walk through the forest.

Tanner makes a face. "No," he says, shrugging. "I guess I didn't. Just kinda stopped turning up." He adjusts the straps of his backpack and wriggles his shoulders beneath them. "They probably assumed I wasn't coming back when they saw us on TV."

"Right." I'm trying to lighten the atmosphere, but ever since I let Sam walk away from the cabin, there has been something separating me from the others. They know I couldn't betray what I'd seen, but that doesn't mean they're okay with it. Tanner might have forgiven me if I'd told him I was on board with his plan to find out if Sam's still out there somewhere, but I can't go along with it just to get him to trust me again.

It's a bad idea. Despite knowing what I do, I can't condone Tanner putting himself at risk like that.

I glance over my shoulder. Nova is walking next to Mack, her arm in his like they're going for a sunny afternoon picnic by the lake.

Too many times in the past few days I've felt like I was going to lose her. After the vision my mother showed us, it's a familiar feeling. The way our ancestors felt when Ava died lives inside us. It has been carried through our bloodlines for generations. It fizzes in our muscles and taints our thoughts. Nova is drawn to us because the part of her that descended from Ava remembers the parts of us that used to love her.

Knowing all of this allowed me to finally understand *why* we were fated to love her, but it did not help me see how we can prevent what has been set in motion.

That I have already seen. In the woods, as we approached the commune, it hit me like a freight train, ripping through the tracks of my body. I saw it all. I saw what would happen to Sam, but I also saw what happens next—to the rest of us.

"I don't want to carry this," I told my mother when I went to say goodbye to her. "I cannot keep it from them. I cannot keep it from *her*."

My mother simply smiled at me and pulled me into her warm embrace. "You will do what you have to, my son." She stepped back and cupped my face in hers. "I believe in you, and you have to believe that you are on the right path. You have to believe it will all be *okay* in the end." Then, sweeping my long hair from my shoulders, she stood on the tips of her toes and kissed my forehead the way she did when I was a boy. "I'm glad you kept your hair long," was the last thing she said to me before I left.

Now, as we march deeper into the forest, the weight of what I know presses heavily on my shoulders. My muscles are throbbing. It has been too long since I kissed Nova or held her close. Too long since she looked at me with love brimming in her un-matching eyes. Too long since I felt the release of exploding inside her, knowing she needs me the way I need her.

I lick my teeth. My canines are slightly more pointed than they should be. Some F.H.B addicts have theirs filed into fangs. Others have prosthetics fitted. I went halfway and had mine shaped. My bites aren't as clean as a vamp's but they're cleaner than they would be without the shaping.

As my thoughts turn to Nova's neck, I screw my eyes shut and try to focus.

I know what's coming, and I should feel soothed by that knowledge. But I don't know what happens between now and then, or how long the between even is. And despite my faith, I don't know how to do what I am expected to do.

"Kole?" Luther's hand arrives on my shoulder. "You okay?"

I nod at him and walk a little faster.

"She'll forgive you eventually." He meets my eyes. "She has to, right? You're bonded. She can't break the bond."

I press my lips together in a tight line and consider the question. "No, she can't break it," I reply. "But she can stretch it so far it sends me over the edge."

Blinking at the darkness in my tone, Luther whispers, "Are you close to going over?"

I flex my fingers at my sides. "Maybe," I tell him. "Luckily, the falls don't offer great access to dealers."

"You have any with you?" Luther asks. He's talking about

F.H.B, asking if I keep a vial on my person for emergencies. I remember the small glass bottle I keep in my desk, the one I was foolish—or smart—enough to leave behind.

"No," I tell him. "But you should watch me with Nova. I don't trust myself when I'm like this. She's not as human as she was, but if she cuts herself or..." I trail off. I thought I was past this. I thought the days of me losing control with her were over.

"You won't hurt her," Luther replies in a matter-of-fact tone. "All this time, you've never hurt her. Even when you drink from her."

"Don't," I snap, turning my gaze to him. "Don't talk about it."

Luther raises his palms. "Alright," he says. "But we're gonna talk about what Tanner suggested this morning, right? 'Cause that shit needs to be talked about."

My breath thickens in my chest. I look up ahead. Tanner's a couple of meters in front, striding in the direction of the falls like they're pulling him toward them. "Maybe he's forgotten about it."

"Forgotten that he offered to drink Nova's blood and jump across dimensions to find Sam?" Luther hisses. "Doubtful, Kole. He *feels* Nova's pain. He's desperate to fix her broken heart. Plus, he and Sam had a different kind of bond. We all saw it."

I bite the inside of my cheek, deliberately applying a little too much pressure with my sharper-than-normal teeth until they draw blood. The bitter taste fills my mouth and I roll my tongue over the pinprick hole, savoring the taste.

"Well, maybe he's realized we should be spending our energy keeping her safe," I say gruffly. As I speak, I know I'm wrong. I know Sam's still a part of this, I just can't believe Tanner's way is how we're supposed to reach him.

Behind us, Nova's voice breaks my train of thought. "Guys," she calls.

Instantly, I spin around, my heart thundering in my chest, ready to run to her if she needs me.

"I think the professor could use a break. He's struggling."

I stride over and put my hand on Mack's upper arm. Nova's right: his brow is clammy and his skin is pale. "We left too soon," I mutter. "We should have stayed until you'd rested properly."

"I'm fine. Just take this for me..." Mack shrugs his pack from his shoulders and I take it. "I'll be fine," he says. "Really."

"Can't we rest for a while?" Nova asks.

"No time." Luther strides over and looks Mack up and down. "Would Snow be faster?" he asks.

Mack rubs his beard and closes his eyes like he's either asking Snow the question or accessing the part of him that *is* Snow to find out the answer. "Not sure we can manage the shift," he says finally. "You go ahead. I'll catch up."

"We aren't leaving you." Nova takes Mack's hand and squeezes it. "No way."

As Nova searches Mack's face, I nudge her arm. At first, she ignores my touch—and the jolt of static electricity that passes between us—but then she looks at me. "You go ahead with Tanner and Luther," I tell her. "I'll stay back here with Baloo."

She opens her mouth to object, but then presses her lips together instead. "Okay," she says tightly. "Fine."

As she strides away from me, ass moving tauntingly from side to side, I sigh and push my fingers through my hair. "Fuck," I breathe, willing The Hunger to subside.

A thump on the back from the professor makes me start walking again. "She'll come back to you," he says quietly. "Just give her time. She's hurting, but she's not gone forever."

I look sideways at him, but he's concentrating on stepping over the raised tree roots beneath our feet.

If only he knew the power of what he'd just said. *She's not gone forever.*

I repeat the words in time with the thud of my steps against the damp earth.

She's not gone forever. She's not gone forever. She's not gone forever.

RAGNOR

"Elena?" The face of the woman I have loved for over twenty-five years blinks up at me. She has been sleeping since she arrived but now—finally—she is awake.

And she is just as perfect as she was then; long dark hair, pale skin, rose-pink lips, and a flash of freckles across the bridge of her nose. I have dreamed of kissing those freckles again for so many nights it seems almost impossible that she is here.

A smile flutters on her perfect lips, but then she frowns and looks down at her stomach. "The baby," she whispers. "Where is the baby?"

My gut twists violently. We have been apart for a quarter of a century and the first thing she thinks of is the child?

"He's being taken care of," I tell her. "You can see him soon."

Elena smiles again. A smile that could light a thousand suns. "Where are we?" she asks, her eyes leaving my face and darting around the room.

"A friend's house," I say softly. "Where you can recuperate in peace."

"And the baby?" she asks again, rubbing her stomach.

The muscles in my jaw tighten. "He's being taken care of," I repeat softly. "You'll see him soon, but you need to recover first, my love. You have been through a lot."

Pushing herself up so she's leaning against the arm of the couch, Elena shivers. I put a cushion behind her then drape a blanket around her shoulders and another over her legs. "Are you hungry?" I ask, stroking the side of her face.

She frowns. "I'm not sure." She rubs her temples and wrinkles her nose. "I have a headache."

"You need to eat," I tell her. "Stay right here. I'll fetch food, and some sweet tea. We'll have you right as rain in no time."

"And then I can see the baby?" she asks, her eyes twinkling.

I force a smile to my lips, then I kiss her forehead as I stand up. "Stay here, Elena," I repeat my instruction, meeting her eyes so she knows I am to be listened to.

Elena nods, then slides down a little and grips the blanket. She closes her eyes. "I'll rest," she says softly. "I'll rest here until you return."

I close the door softly, then release a deep sigh. "Andre!" I shout, although I have no idea if he survived the chaos outside or not. If not, someone else will come.

When Andre does appear, I'm neither pleased nor disappointed to see him.

"Master," he says, tilting his head to display what looks like a vicious burn on the side of his face.

"Fetch food and tea for my wife."

Andre looks past me at the door. If curiosity itches on his tongue, he does not allow it past his lips. "Yes, Master," he says.

He's turning to leave when I snap my fingers.

"Master?" he asks, spinning back to face me.

"Where is Eve?" I ask, squaring my shoulders so I tower above him.

"Outside, Master. She's still outside."

"She's been out there all this time?"

"Yes, she has, Master." Andre licks his lower lip. He looks like a nervous mongrel when he does that.

At the end of the corridor, movement catches my eye. "You!" I shout.

A teenage boy turns toward me. He is uninjured but wide-eyed. "Guard this door," I tell him. "Do not move until I return."

He nods quickly. "Yes, Ragnor," he mutters.

Normally, I'd slap his moon-like face for calling me by my name instead of my title; by now, they should all know to address me as *Master*. But perhaps I'm feeling generous, because instead of reprimanding him I just grunt and stalk toward the front door.

I take the steps two at a time then loop around to the lawn. There is barely any sign of the events that took place last night. The cracks in the lawn have healed themselves, Eve's altar and its ritualistic accoutrements have disappeared, and there is no gaping portal in the sky. In the half-light of the afternoon, everything is still.

Except for Eve.

She is in the distance, pacing back and forth in front of the tree line in her long, flowing dress. Her hair is wild and her arms trembling at her sides. When I reach her, she barely seems to notice I'm here.

I catch her arm. She spins to face me, her eyes nothing more than deep dark pools that make her face seem even smaller. The black veins that betray her filthy F.H.B addiction have spread from the corners of her eyes to the sides of her face. "Ragnor," she whispers, "they have not returned."

I narrow my eyes at her. "Who have not returned?"

Eve hugs herself tightly and shakes her head. "My babies," she whispers. "My poor babies."

"Are you talking about the boys?" I ask, anger swirling like bile in my throat. I thought she'd know better than to mention Nico or Sam in my presence. They are gone and, as far as I'm concerned, they will never be thought of again.

"Boys?" Eve's forehead creases. "Not boys, *beasts*," she says.

I look her up and down. After five years in this witch's presence, I am truly sick of her riddles and her craziness. I am sick of her fragile, willowy frame. I am sick of her sharp angles and her sallow skin. I am sick of fucking her to keep her loyal and of placating her every whim so she doesn't turn on me.

When she provided a link to The King, I dared not upset her. I could never have communicated with him across dimensions if she had not channeled the dark magick necessary to do so. I would not have been able to make the exchange that saw him bring Elena back to me without Eve performing the ritual. But now Elena is back, and my part of the deal is complete. I gave The King what he asked for, and Eve is no longer necessary.

"Beasts?" I ask her, already bored and itching to return to my wife.

"The King's hounds," she says, a sparkle lighting in her dark eyes. "Hellhounds. Beasts that belong to neither dimension… so beautiful, so strong." She jerks her head from side to side and exhales a deep shuddering breath. "He sent them from his world. He sent them into my care. They drank my blood and they came to me. Our babies. Our children. But they're gone. I can't find them."

"Hellhounds?" Something stiffens inside me; I always

believed hellhounds to be a myth. A fairy tale dreamed up to keep young supers in line—behave or the hellhounds will drag you down to the underworld and let you burn.

Eve nods fervently and looks back toward the forest. "They are here for The Phoenix," she says, stepping closer to the trees. "They should have brought her back by now, but they have not returned. What do we do, Ragnor? What do we do?"

Breathing in slowly, I grit my teeth. Then calmly I say, "Eve, The King has the name and location of The Phoenix. Whatever he does next is no concern of mine. I kept my side of the bargain—I found the Fire Bird, I tested her strength, and I restrained myself from being the one to finish her so that *he* might do it himself." I flex my fingers at my sides; it still aggravates me that I was not allowed to end the girl myself. I toyed with the idea of trying to capture her power, and I spent many nights dreaming of the ways in which I could end her pathetic young life when I was done with her.

If I had her power, I wouldn't need The King to create a new world order. I could do it myself. But I wanted Elena more than I wanted the Fire Bird's power. So, I was willing to make the sacrifice he asked of me.

"But he needs our help," Eve says, meeting my eyes. "He needs the hounds to bring her to him and drain her blood so he can rise again. Without her blood—"

"If you want to help him, be my guest," I tell her. "But I want no part of it. The King promised that I will be given a safe place in the new order of things if he returns and that Elena will be by my side. Whatever else is happening, I care not."

"But this is what you wanted," Eve says, grabbing my arm. "You wanted the King to rise, so that humans may become our servants. You wanted the new way of things. You wanted

—" She is rattling off the same spiel I have been giving her, and the rest of the League, for years.

She's right; I do want those things. I believed in the League's mission long before I learned of The Phoenix and The King's plan to return.

But I want my wife more. Now she is home, I truly couldn't give a damn what happens to the rest of the world. I shake Eve loose from me and look back at the house. "I want Elena," I tell her. "Nothing else matters to me now that she is here."

I'm stalking back to the house when I notice my breath pooling in thick clouds in front of me. The air has changed. It is cold, ice-cold.

I turn slowly and look back at Eve. She is kneeling on the ground, and she is surrounded by... *creatures*. Not werewolves—large, gray beasts with ferociously huge heads, dripping jaws, and skin stretched tight over their bones. Hellhounds.

Eve is stroking them, sobbing as they nuzzle into her. "My babies," she cries. "So few of you have returned. Where are your brothers and sisters? What happened to you, my loves?"

Above Eve's head, the air begins to shake. A huge black hole appears, like a rip in the atmosphere. Beyond it, the image that greets me makes me fall to my knees.

"Where is The Phoenix?" the voice of The Shadow King fills the air.

My breath tightens in my chest. I can barely breathe. I gasp and reach for my throat. I see his face. I see him. Not a man, or a demon, or any living thing I recognize.

"Where is The Phoenix?" he roars again.

"She defeated the hounds, my king," Eve cries, waving her arms at the beasts that surround her. "These are all that remain."

A thunderous roar rocks the sky and shakes the mansion.

"Then we will have to try again, won't we?" The King snarls. As the hole grows smaller, and his monstrous image disappears, I hear him add, "Ragnor, do not forget that I can take back what I gave you. You are my servant, and you would do well to remember that."

20

TANNER

When we reach the falls, a wave of comfort washes over me. It has been too long since I was last here, and it takes every ounce of willpower I possess not to run to the water, shed my clothes, and dive beneath the surface.

Instead, I watch Nova's face as she catches her first glimpse of them.

"Remember when I told you I'd bring you here for our first date?" I ask, slipping my hand into hers. "For a swimming lesson?"

Nova looks up at me and smiles. It's genuine; a happy memory from before everything got a little too real. "I was scared of you seeing me in a bathing suit," she says. "But I was telling the truth when I said I can't swim—I really can't."

"Why would you ever be scared of me seeing you in a bathing suit?" I ask, allowing my eyes to travel the length of her body and dance over her curves. From the moment we met, I could think of nothing better than seeing her in as few clothes as possible.

Resting her palm on her chest, she says, "The A.M.A. mark. Remember?"

My nostrils flare. I'm glad Kole covered it before I laid eyes on it. It's bad enough knowing what Johnny did to her, seeing the physical proof might have sent me over the edge.

"No excuses now, though," I whisper, biting her earlobe softly.

Brushing past us, Luther snaps, "We're not here for a trip down memory lane. We need to shield the lake and the falls, then get set up in the caves." He heaves his pack from his shoulders and ditches it on the ground.

Kole, who's been carrying Mack's stuff as well as his own, does the same. His shoulders are big but that doesn't mean they're not aching with the effort of carrying twice the load. "Mack, can you help with the shield?" he asks.

The professor is sitting down on a large, overturned tree trunk. I've often wondered how it got here because it seems too perfectly placed to have occurred naturally. He leans onto his thighs and breathes out heavily. Then he pushes himself to his feet and says, "I'm good. Let's get this place locked down."

Just as we did in the woods around the cabin, we spread out and cast the shielding incantation. After the events of the past few days, it takes a lot out of all of us. Mack in particular looks gray around the edges, and Nova's cheeks flush with the effort.

Glancing at the sky, Luther says, "Who wants to take first watch on the cliffs?"

Kole immediately volunteers. I can sense The Hunger quivering around him. Ever since Nova started trying to push him out of her head, and her heart, he's been struggling to fight The Hunger back. It's like the blood bond between them was the only thing keeping it at bay. But now the bond is stretched and permeable, letting fragments of hunger filter into his soul once more.

"We'll switch at midnight," Luther says. "Six-hour shifts."

Kole nods and stalks away without looking at Nova.

She watches him leave. I don't need to search her aura to know she's pining for him just as much as he's pining for her.

"You can't keep him at arm's length forever," I tell her. "It will make you sick. Denying the blood bond—"

"Fuck the bond," she snaps.

The force of her words, and the anger that vibrates around her as she speaks them, surprises me. Usually, she's so in touch with others' emotions she could almost be an empath herself. But perhaps her grief is clouding her thoughts.

"Nova..." I'm about to tell her I need to talk to her about something when Luther catches my eye.

"The caves," he barks. "Show us the way."

I breathe in slowly, then reluctantly pace out in front.

Luther knows what I want to do, and he's as against it as Kole. So, screw the vote. It's not up to them anymore. It's up to me and Nova. It's her blood and my mind, and therefore it's our decision.

As indignation flares in my stomach, I vow that as soon as we have settled in the caves, I will tell her. I'll tell her that I want to use her blood to find Sam, but there will be no group vote as the others suggested. *She* will have the only vote. She alone will decide whether we try to find her brother.

21

NOVA

The sound of the falls echoes in my ears as we press ourselves to the rocks and slowly edge beneath them. Tanner seems completely at home here; his movements are more relaxed, his smile is brighter, his body more agile.

The caves behind the waterfall are larger than I expected. The first is damp and loud but the second, which we reach through a small narrow tunnel, is quieter and dry enough to light a fire.

"Magick fires only," Tanner says, gesturing to the stone ceiling above our heads. "Nowhere for the smoke to escape."

Luther obliges, waving his hand and casting a large glowing fire in the middle of the cave. Then he sets about unfurling sleeping bags and unpacking our meager food supplies.

Next to the fire, Mack seems a little less uncomfortable. "How are your scratches?" I ask him, pressing the back of my hand to his forehead to make sure he doesn't have a temperature.

"They're much better, Little Star," he says. "Thanks to your nursing. A good night's rest and I'll be good as new tomorrow."

"Good as *old*, you mean," Tanner quips, punching him lightly on the shoulder before fishing some more pink pills from his pocket and telling Mack to swallow them.

As Mack rolls his eyes, I kiss him, then whisper, "I think you're exactly the right amount of old."

"But you *do* think I'm old?" he asks, his dark brown eyes fixing on mine. Leaning in, he whispers, "I hope you're not disrespecting me, Little Star. I'd hate to have to punish you."

A pulse of heat settles between my legs. The moment he finally gave in to me and held me across his lap feels like too long ago. Suddenly, I am desperate for him to overpower me again, so I know he really is okay. So I know his strength has returned.

"You can punish me any time you want to, Daddy." I bite my lower lip, enjoying the small growl that vibrates in Mack's throat, and telling myself he must be okay if he's thinking about fucking me again.

I glance over at Luther. He is watching us with intrigue in his eyes. I shiver, picturing Mack holding me down while Luther uses his flames to torment me again. The heady mixture of pain and pleasure was exactly what I needed. It helped me to forget. It took me somewhere else and reminded me that I am still here.

Before I can straddle Mack's lap and pull his lips to mine, Tanner stands up. The sudden movement makes me look at him. He's bracing his hand on the cave wall. With his other hand, he pushes his fingers through his floppy, dark-blond hair. "Nova," he says loudly, my name bouncing off the cave walls. "I have something to ask you."

"Tanner," Luther says in a tone that makes it sound like a warning.

Tanner ignores him. "It's about Sam," he says quickly.

Immediately, I stand and stride over to him. "What about Sam?" I look up into his eyes. "What about him, Tanner?"

"Do you believe he's still alive?" Tanner searches my face. Something about his expression tells me he's searching my feelings too, but I don't mind. If anything, I *want* him to feel what's inside me.

"Yes," I tell him firmly. "I do, and so does Sarah. She told me she knew all these years that he was still alive and that she feels the same way now."

Tanner nods slowly. "Do you want to know for sure?" he asks.

My mouth drops open a little. When I speak, my voice is barely audible. "Of course, I do. I'd give anything to know if he's still out there." I take Tanner's hand and squeeze it. "If he *is*, it means we stand a chance of getting him back. Doesn't it?"

"No, Nova it doesn't." Luther strides over and puts his hand on my upper arm, tugging me back a little. Staring at Tanner, he says, "Knowing he's out there could be torture for her. Don't you get that? If we find out he's still alive but we can't reach him."

"I'd rather know," I tell him, angling myself so I'm between the two of them. Looking at Tanner, I add, "Is there a way to do that? To find out what happened to him?"

The entire time we have been speaking, Mack has remained silent. Now, he clears his throat and says, "Tanner, dark magick is the only way to communicate with the hell dimensions. We do not have that kind of power."

"What if we do?" Tanner asks, his eyes wide. Moving away from the wall, toward the fire, he says, "We have Nova. We've all seen what her blood does to Kole's powers—it supercharges them, right?"

"Ah ha," Mack nods, watching Tanner carefully.

"So, what if her blood can do the same for me? What if it enables me to jump from our world to the underworld?"

There is a quivering silence. Mack frowns as if he's trying to compute what Tanner's just said. My heart beats fast and hard in my chest. The jump hurt Tanner when he did it before. Surely jumping into *hell* would be too dangerous, right? But he's right—my blood gives Kole extra power. If my blood could do that for Tanner, maybe it wouldn't be dangerous at all.

"You'd do that? For Sam?" I ask, reaching up to cup Tanner's face.

"I'd do it for the both of you," Tanner replies solemnly.

I search his eyes for a long moment. In them, I see no fear just love. No one has ever loved me as fast and as hard as Tanner fell in love with me. Taking my gaze from him, I glance over at Mack. "What do you think, Rhone? Is it too dangerous?"

Mack bites his lower lip, then shakes his head. "I don't know," he says. "I need to think."

"Mack—" Tanner starts to protest, but Mack holds up his hand to stop him.

"I'm not saying no, I'm saying I need some time. My thoughts are fuzzy. I need food and sleep, and so do you three. We've been through a lot, and this is not a decision we should rush into."

I open my mouth to plead with him, but he gives me the same hand-up gesture he gave Tanner.

"If Sam is alive and out there somewhere, nothing is going to change in the next twelve hours." He motions to the fire. "We eat, we sleep, we think. Tomorrow, we talk it through."

"Nova should be the one to decide," Tanner replies quickly.

To my surprise, Mack nods. "Yes, she should be. But in

order to decide, she needs all the facts. We'll each make our case, and she'll have the final say."

I expect Tanner to object again but instead, he nods. "Alright."

Turning to me, Mack says, "We also need to talk about what happened with the truck. Your power is growing, Nova. But we're running out of time to harness it."

Is he trying to tell me we should be focused on magick lessons instead of worrying about whether or not Sam is alive? I study his features. While Kole is stoic, Luther is grumpy, and Tanner wears his heart on his sleeve, Mack is... honest. Straight with me. There is never a double meaning to what he says or a hidden truth.

"Tomorrow," I promise him.

He smiles at me and turns his gaze back to the fire. "Tomorrow."

* * *

I CLOSE my eyes and wriggle down into my sleeping bag, but images of the hellhounds' jaws flash through my brain. I push them away and inch closer to Mack. He is in front of me, Tanner is behind. Luther is by the cave entrance, ready to switch with Kole when it reaches midnight.

As Tanner loops his arms around my waist, I shuffle a little. My ass is against his crotch, and I'm wishing our sleeping bags weren't separating us. Nuzzling into Mack's strong shoulder, I slide my hands down his body. I'm fiddling with the zip on his sleeping bag when he turns around and cups my face in his hands. "Little Star, I can't believe I'm saying this, but I think I need to ask you to try again in the morning. I'm exhausted."

I can't help frowning. Mack has refused me before, but never because he's too tired. Noticing the look on my face, his eyebrows twitch. His gaze flickers to my chest, then he says, "But not too exhausted to watch."

Behind me, Tanner's body has stiffened.

"Perhaps, not too exhausted to give orders?" I ask, biting my lower lip.

Mack's eyes flash amber as he realizes what I'm saying. "Just you? Or do you want company?"

I like the idea of Mack watching me touch myself, but Tanner squeezes my hip and nibbles my ear; there is no way he's going to be left out.

"Company," I reply. "Definitely company."

Instantly, looking over my head at Tanner, Mack barks, "Remove her sleeping bag then undress her."

Tanner grins. "Whatever you say, Professor." Scrambling out of his own sleeping bag, he kneels over me, legs straddling either side of my thighs, and unzips my warm fabric cocoon. As he peels it off me, and cool air meets my hands and feet, I'm not sure I'm warm enough to be stripped completely.

"By the fire," Mack says, as if he's reading my mind. "I want to see her glow."

Obeying Mack's command, Tanner stands, offers me his hand, and pulls me to my feet. Then he positions me as close to the flames as we can get. He's lifting my shirt over my head when I notice Luther moving toward us in the shadows.

"Is this a private party or can anyone join in?" he asks darkly as he stares at me from the other side of the fire. Through the flames, he looks deliciously dangerous; flickering shadows decorating his deep, ochre skin.

Tanner and I both look at Mack. He has climbed out of his sleeping bag and is sitting with his back against the cold cave wall, knees drawn up but wide enough apart for me to see the outline of the large bulge in his pants. There's a pause while he stares at the three of us, then he mutters, "Did you pack any rope, Luther?" His tone is so gravely it scrapes my skin on impact. Just the word *rope* sends a flutter of nervous excitement to settle between my legs.

Without hesitating, as Tanner continues obeying Mack's instruction to undress me, Luther strides to his pack and pulls out a large bundle of blue rope. I have no idea why he brought it, but the very sight of him carrying it toward me makes my mouth instantly dry.

When I'm naked, Tanner nods approvingly and adjusts himself. He's in dark gray boxers, his top half illuminated by the fire, shadows emphasizing the dips and grooves in his muscular physique. "May I touch her?" he asks Mack politely, his fingers twitching at his sides.

"Only her arms," Mack replies.

"Arms only," Tanner whispers, running his hands over my skin, leaving a shiver in their wake.

"Enough," Mack barks just as Tanner's about to lean down and kiss the inside of my wrist.

For a moment, no one moves. Luther is on one side of me, holding his large cord of rope. Tanner is on the other, arms at his sides. I realize they're waiting for Mack to tell them what to do.

"Tie her up," Mack says. "Breasts, wrists, crotch."

My eyes widen. I turn to Luther and he meets my gaze, inching a little closer. I take in the rope, and how good Luther's strong fingers look curled around it, then I nod—almost imperceptibly—because I know he needs me to tell him it's okay.

As soon as I give him a signal that I'm willing to surrender myself, Luther spins me to face Tanner and begins winding the dark blue rope around my body. I have no idea *how* he knows how to do this. Is he making it up? It doesn't *seem* like he's making it up.

"Loop this under her breasts," he tells Tanner.

With hesitant hands, Tanner does as Luther says. "I've never done this before," he says, his fingers purposefully brushing my erect nipples as he moves the rope over them and begins tying it around me.

"Me neither," I whisper.

Gaining confidence, Tanner winds the blue rope under my breasts and around my back, then I feel it crisscross and return to my front. "Good," Luther says, gesturing to my breasts. "Now pull it up between them and over her shoulders."

"Like this?" Tanner asks.

"Perfect." Luther disappears from my line of sight. He's behind me; I can feel his heat. Suddenly, he tugs my arms back so my shoulder blades are straining toward one another Then he grabs the rope Tanner hooked over my shoulders, tugs it down, and binds my wrists too. After my wrists, the rope returns to my waist. Then he almost braids it, so it's a little thicker, and tells me to open my legs. Without my hands to steady myself, I lean into Tanner's large steady chest as Luther pulls the rope under my crotch then joins it to the ties at my wrists.

Only my legs and feet can move freely. The rest of my body is completely bound and exposed. I can barely breathe. I'm completely at their mercy. They could do whatever they want to me now, and I couldn't stop them. Knowing this, but knowing I can trust them completely, is a new kind of pleasure.

When Luther has finished tying me up like a Christmas present, he turns me to face Mack. He tugs on the back of the rope, and the friction between my legs makes me hum.

"Good," Mack says. "Nova, I think you should say thank you." He licks his lower lip.

"Thank you," I whisper.

"Not like that," he says. "On your knees. Mouth open."

Unsteady without the use of my hands and arms, I sink awkwardly to my knees. I turn toward Luther's crotch but Mack snaps, "Facing me. Mouth open. Tongue out."

I do as he says. Stretching my mouth as wide as I can, I stick out my tongue and wait.

22

MACK

Nova is completely at our mercy. Seeing her like this fills me with a hedonistic mixture of pride and lust. "Good girl," I tell her. Then I look at the boys. "Luther, you first."

I sit back and watch as Luther frees his pierced cock from his pants. He's not quite hard, but the second he slaps his shaft onto Nova's tongue, he stiffens beautifully.

"Keep still," I tell her. "You are here for them."

She whimpers, but excitement dances in her eyes as Luther rubs his metal-studded cock over her lips and tongue. When she has moistened it nicely for him, he grips the back of her head and slams into her mouth so hard she gags. The sound she makes sends a vibration of arousal to my dick.

Luther thrusts into her mouth three times, hard, before slowing up. Saliva drips from her mouth. This time, he's more tender, stroking her lips with his glistening tip. Like the good girl she is, she flicks her tongue over his piercings.

"Do they taste good?" I ask her. "Does Luther's metal taste good?"

She makes a small *mm hmm* sound, but it's muffled by Luther's cock.

"I can't hear you," I bark.

Luther removes his dick just long enough for Nova to say, "Yes, Daddy, he tastes good."

Behind her, Tanner looks almost ready to blow already. He hasn't taken his boxers off or touched his dick, but he's practically shaking with desire as he watches her.

"Tanner feels left out," I tell her.

Immediately, she turns her face to Tanner. Her arms twitch as if she's forgotten they're tied behind her back and was going to use her hands to free him from his boxers. He does it for her then, more tenderly than Luther, he eases his dick into her waiting mouth.

While Tanner strokes her head and whispers things I can't hear, Luther kneels in front of her and tweaks her rose-red nipple with his index finger. "Her buds are perfect," he says, flashing me a grin that says he knows how much I want one in my mouth.

"Taste them for me," I tell him.

Dipping his head, Luther seals his mouth around her left nipple. He's sucking hard, making her hum onto Tanner's cock, when he starts to tug on the rope. He jerks it gently, applying just the right amount of pressure to her cunt.

I watch as she starts to grind her hips down onto it, mewing at the friction on her swollen clit. Panting, she releases Tanner from her mouth and says, "Please, someone fuck me."

"Don't be impatient," I growl. "You'll be fucked when we decide you will be fucked." Then I tell Luther, "Stand up. She's going to take you both at the same time."

Luther does as I say. Together, he and Tanner slide their dicks across Nova's lips, teasing her tongue, her cheeks, and her chin. She laps desperately at them, trying to catch both at the same time.

"Tanner, put your hand around Luther's shaft." I have no idea how my instruction will go down. Tanner has fucked Kole, and Luther has fucked Kole, but as far as I know, they've never fucked each other. However, I do know that seeing them touch each other will drive Nova crazy with lust.

Luther tilts his head but doesn't react as Tanner follows my orders. He curls his large fingers around Luther's cock, then squeezes. Luther twitches in his hand, then, without being asked, takes hold of Tanner in return.

As they fist each other's dicks, they take turns stopping and plunging into Nova's mouth. She groans desperately, wriggling her hips to try and find the smallest amount of pressure for her aching clit.

"Bring her to me," I tell them.

Lost in the moment, it takes them a few seconds to respond.

"Bring her to me," I repeat. Tanner's the first to listen. He lets go of Luther's cock and helps Nova up from the floor. Taking her elbow, he guides her toward me. "Turn her around and sit her in my lap."

Tanner does as I say. Gently, he spins Nova so she's facing away from me then, as I straighten my legs, he helps her lower herself into my lap.

"We're going to watch a show together, Little Star," I whisper in her ear.

Without asking permission, Tanner bends down and kisses her hard on the lips. I think about telling him off, but let it go because the way she murmurs as his lips leave hers makes my dick throb in my pants.

"Tell them what you want to see," I whisper in her ear.

Nova stiffens. Her entire body tenses, and I find myself wishing I wasn't wearing pants so I could feel how wet she is.

Luther and Tanner are standing in front of us, silhouetted by the crackling flames, their impressive erections throbbing with the need to come. Nova hesitates. She breathes in slowly then, in a commanding voice that makes my balls pulse, she says, "Luther, show Tanner what it's like to have a pierced dick in his mouth."

Tanner cocks his head at her, surprised and excited at the same time, then quickly sinks to his knees. Without hesitating, Luther grabs Tanner by the hair and jerks into his mouth.

As we watch them, I moisten my fingers with my tongue, then slide my hands up Nova's body, over the curve of her hips and her stomach, then begin to toy with her nipples. She strains against the rope, desperate to move her arms. When she does, I jerk the rope between her legs. "Keep still," I growl.

The whimpering sound that leaves her mouth makes me smile and return to her nipples.

As we watch, Luther tips his head back and braces his hands on his neck so his elbows are jutting out sideways and his muscles bulge. He releases a loud throaty groan. He's ready to come, but it's not Tanner who should swallow it.

"Stop," I tell them. With a noise that makes it sound almost painful, Luther removes his cock from Tanner's mouth and starts to fist it almost urgently. I slide my hand up and take hold of Nova's throat. I apply pressure, just enough to make her moan. "Give it to her," I tell Luther. "She wants to swallow it. Don't you, Little Star?"

Without hesitating, Luther strides over. I flex my fingers around Nova's neck, encouraging her to open her mouth. When she does, Luther jerks into it. He comes quickly and violently, spraying ropes of hot cum to the back of her throat. I feel her swallow it; feel her muscles contracting beneath my fingers.

"Do you want more?" I ask her, my lips teasing her earlobe.

She nods and looks at Tanner. "Please," she says. "Please give me more."

As Luther stands aside, Tanner moves slowly toward her. He strokes the side of her face, then eases his cock into her waiting mouth. Hungrily, she laps and sucks and hums onto his shaft until he yells, "Fuck, Nova!" and an orgasm shakes his body.

Nova is shaking too. She swallows again, then leans back onto my chest. "Please," she says, jerking her shoulders. "Please, let them untie me, Daddy."

I meet Tanner's eyes and nod.

Quickly, he and Luther pull her to her feet and unfasten the knots binding her in place. Despite myself, I'm rock hard, and the spot at the base of my dick is pulsing.

When she's free, she rubs her wrists, shakes her arms, then stands completely still waiting for me to tell her what's next.

"Who do you want to fuck, Little Star?" I ask.

"I'll do whatever you say," she replies in a tone that's hot as hell.

"You've been a good girl tonight," I tell her. "So, you can choose."

She glances at Luther and then at Tanner. Both are seconds away from being ready to go again, but her eyes return to me. Without saying anything, she walks toward me, voluptuous hips swaying in the firelight. She bends down, giving Tanner and Luther a prime view of her ass, and hooks her fingers into the waistband of my pants. She pulls them down only just far enough to free my waiting erection, then she positions her feet on either side of my hips and brings my mouth to her cunt.

Gripping her perfectly round ass, I flick my tongue over her swollen clit. She is unbelievably wet, and when I slide two fingers up inside her, she groans and braces her palms on the wall behind me.

"Don't stop," she murmurs, grinding against my mouth. "Don't stop, Daddy."

Hearing her call me that makes me groan onto her clit. The vibration of my lips makes her cry out, then sink quickly to her knees. She hovers above me, then takes hold of my cock and drags my head across her slit.

"Fuck, Nova." I dig my nails into her hips, then run my hands up her back.

Finally, she slides onto me.

"Be gentle," I whisper. "I was supposed to be watching."

"Oh, I'm sorry." She sits up, taking her heat away from me. "I'll stop."

"Don't you fucking dare." I grab her and slam her back down, groaning loudly as she starts to ride me.

As she moves up and down, Tanner's hands appear from behind. He's lifting her beasts toward my open mouth, offering me her nipples, guiding them to my tongue. As I suck and nibble at them, I scratch deep grooves in her perfectly smooth back. She cries out as the pain merges with pleasure.

With one hand on my good shoulder, she reaches her other hand down between us and leans back so she can play with her clit. Luther catches her face with his hands and steals a kiss from her waiting lips.

I am lapping at her nipples, Tanner holding her breasts so they're pushed together right in front of my lips, when her skin begins to sparkle. It's a sight I've seen countless times before, and yet it still takes my breath away.

As her orgasm builds, tiny orange sparks float from her and swirl into the air. Luther stands back, watching as if she's the most beautiful thing he's ever seen.

She grabs my face, lifts my chin, and kisses me. It's a searching, passionate, loving kiss that makes my entire body tense as my orgasm thunders toward me. She moans into my mouth, the sound of her pleasure wrapping itself around my tongue.

Grinding down, applying one last shudder of friction to her core, she jerks forward as she starts to come. Our bodies slam together. Her back arches, then she closes her eyes and scrapes her fingers through her hair, elbows out to the sides, breasts perfectly illuminated by the fire. A spark flickers on her right nipple. I catch it with my tongue, and she shudders. Then she holds her arms out, like a bird taking flight, and sighs.

"I'm glad you caved," she says, lowering her arms and smiling as she meets my eyes.

"Is that a joke?" I ask, brushing her hair from her shoulders and looking pointedly at our surroundings.

She shrugs, a bubble of laughter shaking her chest.

"It's a terrible joke." Tanner kisses her forehead.

"Truly terrible." Luther offers her his hand and helps her up.

"I have other talents apart from humor," she quips.

"You certainly do." Tanner is still drinking in her body. Inching closer, he slips his hand between her legs then raises a moist finger and says, "You need to clean up, Little Star. The professor's made you rather messy."

"Luckily, there's a big old lake outside." She lingers for a moment, then turns and runs from the cave. Like a couple of big kids, Luther and Tanner look at me for permission to chase after her.

"Go," I tell them. "She shouldn't be out there alone."

"Yes, Sir." Tanner offers me a mock salute, winks, then scampers out of the cave after Nova with Luther close at his heels.

23

LUTHER

Seeing Nova smiling brings an uncharacteristic lightness to my chest. Perhaps she's smiling because of what we just did, but I think it's more likely she's buoyed by the idea that Tanner might be able to find Sam. That her foster brother might not be gone forever.

I wish I believed that Tanner's plan would result in something other than disaster, but even if it works and we discover where Sam is—even if Tanner is somehow able to jump across dimensions and talk to him—what then? How do we get him back? Wouldn't knowing that he was out there and being unable to help him drive Nova into an even darker spiral of grief than the one that has consumed her since he disappeared?

I follow them into the water. Nova reminds Tanner she can't swim, and he scoops her into his arms. I stand with the cold water lapping my waist, watching her naked body in the moonlight. Gently, Tanner lowers her into the lake, and she squeals at the icy temperature. I splay my fingers and rest my palms on the surface, sending a wave of warmth toward her.

Realizing what I'm doing, she does the same, and soon the

three of us are surrounded by steam. Like we're bathing in a hot spring, we splash soothing water onto our arms and chests, and let it wash away the remnants of our activities in the cave.

"Did you like being at our mercy?" I ask, slipping my hands around her naked waist, enjoying how smooth her skin is when it's being kissed by lake water.

"I did, actually," she says, eyebrow raised as she tilts her head back and kisses me. She strokes the side of my face and smiles. "A few months ago, the thought of being that vulnerable would have terrified me. But I trust you." She turns and pulls Tanner toward her, kissing him too. "All of you."

For a moment, Tanner sinks into her kiss, but then he pulls away and glances up at the cliffs. I know what he's thinking; he's thinking of Kole.

Nova understands, too, because she shakes her head, sending beads of moisture flying from the end of her bedraggled tresses.

"It's eating him up, you know," Tanner says softly, still looking in the direction of Kole's outpost at the top of the falls.

"I know." Nova sighs heavily and brushes her palm across her tattooed chest.

"He would have told you if he could," I mutter, tightening my grip on her waist so she knows I'm serious.

"I know," she says again before sinking into silence.

For a few long, delicious minutes, Tanner and I float in the warm water, kissing Nova's lips and shoulders, enjoying the feel of holding her between us. Then Tanner surprises me by stealing a kiss from my mouth instead of hers. He grips the back of my head while his hot tongue hungrily explores.

Nova hums gently, and strokes each of our faces. "That's so fucking delicious," she breathes. "Do it again."

But as Tanner's lips meet mine, a sharp wind blows across

the surface of the lake and the warmth instantly disappears from the water.

Nova yelps and starts to shiver. "Luther, what happened?"

I look at my hands, willing the heat to return, but it doesn't.

Then... a voice fills the air, zipping past us on the breeze, curling around our bodies. *The werewolf. Find the werewolf. Fated to five. Find the werewolf. Fated to five. Find the werewolf.*

Nova spins around, splashing the surface of the lake with her outstretched arms. Her eyes wide, she looks from me to Tanner. "Did you hear that? Did you hear it?"

Tanner nods slowly. I swallow hard and rub my palm over my head. The others have talked about a 'voice' telling them what to do, but I thought it was all wrapped up in the fact Kole is a seer, Tanner is an empath, and Nova's whatever *she* is.

Now that I've heard it for myself, my head is spinning.

Nova wriggles free from us, finds her footing, and strides through the water to the lake's edge. She doesn't look back but breaks into a run and heads for the caves.

Tanner and I exchange a worried glance, then follow her. By the time we reach the cave, she's pulling on her clothes and speaking quick-fire at Mack.

"I'm not waiting until morning. The voice told us to find Sam. *Fated to five* is what it said. That means we need him. Whatever's about to happen, we need him." She spins to face us as we pick up our pants and shirts and hurriedly get dressed.

"She's right," I tell Mack. "I heard it too."

"And it told you to find Sam?"

"Find the werewolf," Tanner says, combing his wet floppy hair with his fingers. "Fated to five, find the werewolf."

Gingerly, Mack stands up, using the cave wall to steady himself. "Alright," he says. "Then we better get Kole. If we're doing this, we're doing it together." He fixes his gaze on Tanner. "If it goes wrong, it'll take all four of us to bring you back."

Tanner nods in agreement, even though he must be thinking the same thing I am; if this goes wrong, we might not be able to bring him back from where he ends up.

* * *

When I go to fetch Kole, he looks up from his post as if he's expecting me.

"You heard it too?" I ask.

He nods solemnly, rubbing his long dark beard. "I did."

"We're doing it now." I shake my head, then rub my palms over my face. "Fuck, Kole, I heard the voice. I know Nova wants this but..." I meet his eyes and stare deep into them. "Will Tanner be okay? Have you seen what happens?"

Kole sighs heavily. His tattooed upper arms, visible from beneath his black t-shirt, twitch as he clenches his fists. "Tanner will be okay," he says.

I move closer, studying his face in the eerie light of the moon.

"I am telling the truth," he says bluntly. "Tanner will survive the jump. I'm not sure what it will do to him, but I know he'll survive."

I want to ask why he's able to tell me this but couldn't tell us about Sam, but I don't. Seer laws are complex, and I won't even try to pretend I understand them.

"Alright then," I tell him. Clearly, neither of us is going to mention the fact that Tanner *surviving* isn't necessarily a good thing if he ends up completely fucked up. The way he was when we first found him. Or worse. "Mack wants us all there."

Kole nods solemnly. "After you," he says, motioning to the

rocky path that leads down the side of the falls back to the lake.

When we reach the bottom, the others are waiting. Nova is moving from foot to foot as if she's standing on hot coals. Tanner is in the distance, stock still, face tilted toward the moon. Mack is sitting on the upturned log, staring out at the lake.

"We're here," I announce, even though they know that already. "Is Tanner ready?"

Mack looks over at him. He's still staring up at the moon. I move toward Nova and put my arm around her in an attempt to ease her jumpiness.

"Did anyone bring a knife?" I ask, the question sticky and uncomfortable in my mouth.

"A knife?" Nova swallows hard.

"It'll need to be more than a pin-prick this time," Kole says darkly. "Not like in the cellar."

Nova's fingers move to the scar on her upper arm. The one we all know Johnny gave her but haven't dared to imagine how or why. "I'm not sure I can let you cut me like that." She shudders and curls her arms around her own waist.

"Alright, we don't need to use a knife." Kole moves slowly toward her. I step away, allowing them to move into each other's orbit. Barely an inch away from him, Nova inhales sharply—I can practically hear the power of the bond they share throbbing on her skin. Kole runs his tongue over his teeth. "Did you ever wonder how I was able to puncture your skin so easily?"

Nova stares up at him, her eyes moving to his half-open mouth.

"My teeth were shaped when I was with the League." Slowly, as if he's worried he might startle her, Kole brushes her damp hair from her shoulder and runs his index finger down her neck. "Do you still trust me?" he asks, his dark eyes boring into hers.

She breathes in, her chest rising slowly. There is a stretched moment of silence between them then she closes her eyes and nods. "Yes, I do."

Kole's features twitch. His eyes soften, and a low rumble comes from deep in his throat before he says, "Then I will bite, and Tanner will drink. No knife." He takes his hand away from her, even though it's obvious that everything in his body is telling him to keep her close.

Nova's fingers brush Kole's upper arm. "Okay," she says. "I'm okay with that."

From a little way down the beach, Tanner calls, "I'm ready."

24

NOVA

Luther lights a fire on the beach by the lake, and we sit in a semi-circle around it. After hearing the voice for himself, he seems to have accepted what's about to happen, but I can tell he is still worried.

"She'll be safe, won't she?" he asks Kole.

Before Kole can answer, I squeeze Luther's hand. "All Tanner needs is my blood. He's the one who's at risk, not me." I stroke his palm with my index finger. I know he's remembering Thessaly's vision. I know he's thinking of The Original Six and their pain at losing Ava. But I am not Ava, and I'm not going anywhere.

Angling myself toward Kole, I brush my hair from my neck and tell him, "Go ahead."

He is kneeling, scratching his thighs with his fingernails. For the second time, a low rumble comes from deep in his chest. He moistens his lower lip and his eyes darken.

"Kole, can you do this?" Tanner asks. "The Hunger is strong right now. Are you sure you can?"

Flashing his eyes at Tanner, Kole snaps, "No blade will

touch her skin. I will do it." Then he wraps a bulky arm around my waist and pulls me toward him.

As always, I feel small and vulnerable in his grasp. The familiar mix of excitement and fear swirls inside me. It has been too long since I was close to him and, now I'm in his arms again, my entire body wants to surrender to him. Every fiber of my being tells me that I am his, and he is mine, and that he can do whatever he wants to me.

Instead of sinking his teeth into my neck, Kole turns my face toward him and steals a long lingering kiss. I sigh into his mouth. Despite everything, I still love him. I still need him.

His large hands explore my back as he lifts me onto his lap. I wrap my legs around his waist, and his lips move from my neck to my chest. They travel across my chest, licking my collarbone, caressing the raised skin beneath the tattoo he gave me.

When I am sighing, wet, and desperate for more of him, he smooths my hair away and exposes the pulsing vein on my neck. Without warning, his teeth sink into me. As they puncture my skin, I cry out and grab the back of his head.

I want him to drink from me. I want to feel him sucking and lapping and devouring me, but with a roar that makes it sound like it's physically painful for him to do so, he pulls away and pushes me toward Tanner instead.

Wiping his mouth, and panting, Kole sits back and digs his fingers into the sand on either side of him. Mack and Luther move to take hold of his arms as if they're worried The Hunger will take over and he'll be unable to stop himself from coming for me.

He watches with wide, ink-black eyes as blood trickles down my throat. It drips down between my breasts, causing Kole to shudder and slam his eyes closed.

Tanner approaches me slowly. He stares at the bite on my

neck, then looks at Kole. "How much?" he asks. "How much should I drink…?"

"Until you feel your magick growing," Kole replies, eyes still closed. "Drink until you feel her blood changing you."

Kneeling in front of Tanner, I brush his hair from his face and kiss the bridge of his nose. "It's alright," I tell him, meeting his eyes. "we're doing this for Sam."

"Not just for Sam," he says softly. "The voice said we need him. We're doing this for all of us."

I nod and slot my fingers between his. "For all of us." I slide my other hand around the back of his neck and bring his lips toward my neck.

I feel the warmth of his breath on my skin, then his tongue. He licks the blood from my chest and follows it up toward the leaking wound Kole left behind. Then he seals his lips over the holes and begins to suck.

The sensation makes me gasp. My eyes widen, and I press on the back of his head, urging him closer. At first, he is gentle, but then he is not. He grips my shoulders hard and sucks even harder. I feel his teeth grazing my skin, his hands move to my waist, and he pulls me down beneath him, arching over me, pinning my arms to the ground, his body pressed against mine as he continues to drink.

"Tanner…" Kole's voice reaches me, but Tanner doesn't stop. "Tanner, that's enough."

Finally, gasping for breath, Tanner drags his mouth away from my neck. Blood drips down his chin and stains his teeth. "Fuck," he breathes, standing up and staggering away from me. "Fuck!"

Leaving Kole with Luther, Mack moves to my side and helps me sit up. "Are you okay, Little Star?" he brushes a gentle finger over the wound on my neck. I can feel the blood drying on my skin already.

I nod at him and lean into his arms. "I'm okay, but is Tanner?"

Tanner yells and punches the air. "By the stars and the moon... fuck!" He is smiling and his eyes are bright. He runs to Kole and punches him on the shoulder. "Why didn't you *tell* me it felt like that?"

Kole stands up and grabs hold of Tanner's shoulders, trying to center him.

Tanner tilts his head and stares up into Kole's face. "Fuck, Kole. I can see you." He narrows his eyes, reaching out to trace Kole's jaw with his index finger. "I see inside you. All of it. Every piece. All the memories." He frowns a little. "All the *darkness*."

At that, Kole lets go and steps back a few paces. "If you're going to attempt the jump, do it now while the power is strongest."

As if he'd forgotten why we started this in the first place, Tanner becomes suddenly more stoic and says, "Right. The jump. Sam." Then he claps his hands, rubs them together, and shouts, "I'm coming for you, buddy. Don't worry. I'm coming."

* * *

While my blood turns Kole into The Hulk, it seems to have turned Tanner into an overexcited teenager. He's practically giddy, fizzing with the high of the emotions he's feeling. Even the darker ones. Striding toward the lake, he sits down in the shallow water so it almost covers his thighs, and crosses his legs. Placing his palms on either side of his hips, he wriggles his fingers into the sand, then he tilts his head from side to side.

"Do you need a blindfold?" I ask, not daring to get too close.

Tanner shakes his head. "Not this time, Little Star. Not this time."

Then he starts to chant. The words are familiar, although I still don't know what they mean. We watch as he repeats them over, and over, and over.

Just when I'm starting to think something's wrong, and that it's not going to work, his head snaps back. His eyes are bright. They shimmer and glow, and then a white light fills them. The same white light bleeds from his fingertips into the lake, shooting like lightning rods across its surface.

Tanner opens his mouth and roars at the sky. The light crackles up and down his body like static electricity. His legs twitch. His arms lift up, water dripping from his palms. Then his entire body lifts with it.

"Holy hell." I jump to my feet and run toward him, but Mack catches me and tugs me back.

"Nova, don't." Kole slams an arm in front of my stomach to keep me from ducking out of Mack's grasp.

The three of us watch as Tanner rises up into the air, arms splayed at his sides, lightning dancing up and down his body then down into the lake and across the water.

Overhead, thunder rumbles through the sky. Dark clouds move quickly, obscuring the moon and stars and casting the lake into almost complete darkness—except for Tanner's light.

He starts to move. He floats out to the lake's center. Below him, the water begins to glow. As if there's a fire somewhere at the bottom of the lake, a ball of dancing light flickers beneath him.

He roars again, clenching his fists. Then so quickly I barely understand what's happening, the light drags him under.

25

TANNER

I feel fucking amazing. Like I could swim the Atlantic Ocean barely needing to stop for breath. Like I could make love to Nova for hours, days, weeks. Like I'm invincible.

Light courses through me. It fills me up and jumps from my body, creating an unbreakable bond between me and the lake's power.

I've always known the falls were powerful. I've always known they were important, but now I *feel* them. They speak to me. The heart of the lake speaks to me. I move closer to her—to the lake—floating through the air like a fucking eagle.

She's pulling me toward her, giving me her power.

But then she drags me under. Water fills my lungs. I can't breathe. I can't scream. I can't see. Everything is black. The white light has disappeared, and cold dark water presses down on me.

Pain replaces the giddy pleasure I felt a few moments ago. Unbearable pain, like my bones are snapping and molten lead burns in the spaces between them. I grab my skull, digging my fingernails into my scalp, screaming as blinding pain rolls through my head, down my neck, and spine, and into my feet.

When my vision starts to clear, I see a large stone-flagged room. Some kind of hall. There is a throne in front of me, but it is empty. I claw at the ground and cry, "Please, not again. Please, make it stop."

Then I'm no longer in the throne room, I'm in a basement. A figure strides toward me, silhouetted in the darkness. The sight of him sends waves of fear through my body.

As the figure shows his face, and I scramble back, pressing myself against the wall behind me, I realize I am *not* me. I am Sam.

This is Sam's memory, which means I made it; I am inside his head.

I try to take in his surroundings, but they are moving in and out of focus. They're not real. He's not really here; he is stuck inside the memory. When it ends, there is no time to take a breath. It restarts. The same man, the same fear, the same pain.

I feel it all as if it is happening to me but, as well as my own pain, I feel Sam's. I start to claw at my head. I need to get out of here. I need to get out. I can't see it again.

Sam screams. I scream too. Then the blinding light is back. I feel water rushing around me. Cold fills me up. I start to shiver. I can't breathe. My lungs are tight, burning with the need for air.

Then suddenly, I'm free. I'm gasping for breath. Something is holding onto me. I thrash and writhe in the water. My hand meets something large and wet. I realize teeth are gripping my shirt, pulling me toward the shore.

"Snow?" I splutter.

The huge white bear grunts and keeps on pulling. When we reach the beach, he drags me onto the sand and drops me from his jaws. Nova rushes to me, smoothing her hands over my sodden clothes, then my hair, then my face. She jerks my head toward her and stares into my eyes.

"Are you there? Are you safe?" she asks, tears streaming down her cheeks.

Snow shakes his large body, sending droplets of water flying, then quickly shifts back into Mack. The professor kneels down next to me. "Tanner? What happened?"

Luther and Kole are close too. Luther waves his hand and conjures a flame, which he casts sweeping over my body to dry my wet skin.

"He's alive." I look at each of them in turn. "I found him."

"Where?" Nova asks, gripping my hand so tightly the pressure whitens her knuckles.

"He's stuck. In his memories." I meet Nova's eyes and a shudder of fear drips through me. "He's there, Nova. But I have no idea where *there* is. And I have no idea how we're going to get him out."

* * *

WE'RE BACK in the caves behind the falls. It's nearly daybreak but, all the same, Luther has taken Kole's spot up on top of the falls. The extra shift has left the professor exhausted, and he's sleeping by the fire. Only me, Nova, and Kole are awake.

She is sitting between us—the tip of our triangle—with a hand on each of our thighs. Kole hands me a mug of hot valerian-laced tea. As he does, his face shimmers. The cave dips in and out. Flashes of light scorch my eyes. Then everything is normal again. At least, for now.

Both of them watch me for a moment, not pressing me for details, just staring at me as if they're worried I might disintegrate.

Finally, I say, "I'm not sure what to do now. I found him, but what I saw... I don't know how it helps."

"Talk us through it again," Nova says, tucking her knees up in front of her and wrapping her arms around them.

For the second time, I tell them what I saw and what I felt; the hall, the figure, the pain. "He was crouched underneath some stairs. In a basement. The guy came for him."

"His foster father," Nova mutters. "It had to be his foster father. The one who sold him to *Spine*."

"Wherever he is, he's reliving his worst memories." I shake my head, but the movement sends a sharp pain to my temples. I suck in a deep breath then add, "I need to go back. I need to stay longer, so I can figure out where exactly he is and how to bring him back."

I expect Nova to be nodding. Instead, she looks at Kole with worry etched around her eyes.

Kole puts a firm hand on my shoulder. "Rest. We'll talk about when you've slept."

I'm about to object when Nova stands up, fetches a sleeping bag, and tells me to get inside it. "If we're going to try again, you need to rest," she says, crouching to kiss my forehead. When I'm inside the sleeping bag, she takes my mug of half-drunk tea and places it by the fire. Then she strokes my cheek and whispers, "Sleep now. We'll figure it out, but sleep now."

26

KOLE

Nova and I move into the cave just behind the falls. She leans on the slick rocky wall and stares out past the fast-moving water. Her free hand goes to her neck and traces the mark that Tanner and I left on her.

I'm calmer now I have tasted her. It took every ounce of willpower I possessed to stop myself from pushing Tanner out of the way so I could taste her myself, but the act of her surrendering herself to me again—forgiving me—has satiated The Hunger. At least, for now.

"He's not okay," I tell her. "I've seen him like this before."

"After he found us both at the hotel?" she asks. "Or the first time he found Sam?"

I shake my head. "Neither."

The sound of the water tumbling over the rocks mimics the sensation in my veins when I look at her, so I look away.

"When I first found Tanner, he was being held captive by the League. He was with them for fifteen years. They took him when he was at college, sealed him in a concrete prison, and deprived him of water so they could amplify his empathic talents."

Nova takes a sharp breath. "He never told me that."

"I had a vision. I was high, living in Europe at the time. I called Mack and Luther and told them we had to rescue him."

"Why?" she asks softly. "Why did you feel like you had to do that?"

"Because I knew he was part of the prophecy, just like you know Sam is part of it." I glance sideways at her. Shadows of dancing water move across her face. "The League taught him how to jump into other peoples' heads. Humans and supers. They used Tanner to help them track and manipulate their victims. Worse, sometimes. My hunch is they hoped he could one day find *you*, but jumping only works if you already know the identity of the person."

"I had no idea. Fifteen years? How is he so… okay?" Nova looks back in the direction of the orange glow coming from the second cave.

"He wasn't. For a long time, he had trouble keeping his grasp on reality." I pause, wondering how much information she needs about exactly how I managed to pull Tanner back from the brink. "I was suffering too. Recovering from the F.H.B. That was when Luther built the cabin. It became a kind of therapy. The four of us going out into the woods to work on it together."

Nova steeples her fingers together and turns to face me. "You're worried Tanner's going to return to how he was before?"

"Wherever he's just been, it took more power than he's ever had access to before. Who knows what will happen if he tries it again."

As Nova's eyes moisten, and she presses her lips together in an attempt to keep her tears inside, I open my arms. She stares at them for a moment then, with a heavy sob, falls into them. Clinging to my upper arms, she whispers, "I'm sorry. I'm so sorry. I shouldn't have blamed you."

"It's alright, Little Star." My muscles sigh at the sensation of having her close again. I feel her heart beating against my chest and breathe in her scent. "It's alright."

"I missed you," she sniffs. "But I miss Sam too. So much." She stares up at me, her cheeks wet and flushed, her fingers gripping my shirt. "What do we do? The voice said we need Sam, but how can we get him back without putting Tanner at risk again?"

"I don't know." I kiss the tears on her left cheek. "I promise you; I'm telling the truth when I say I don't know." I move my lips to her right cheek and kiss the wetness there too.

Nova closes her eyes and slides her hands up my chest to loop around my neck. Then she finds my mouth and presses her warm lips to mine. Cupping her face with my hands, I allow my tongue to caress hers. I feel her nipples stiffen against my chest and tug her closer.

Frantically, she reaches for my shirt. She pulls it up over my head and tosses it to the floor, then runs her fingertips over my stomach, following the dips and grooves of my muscles. She kisses my shoulders, trails her tongue over my ink, then removes her own shirt.

She's not wearing a bra. I put my hands on her arms and make her stand still while I savor the sight of her, then I lower my head and swirl my tongue over her waiting pink buds.

Nova lets out a small mewing sound, then tugs at my belt. She unfastens it quickly and shoves my pants down until my erection springs free. She doesn't look at it, doesn't touch it, just presses her hands on my shoulders and stares into my eyes. *Fuck me, Kole. Please, fuck me.*

For the first time in days, her voice fills me up. With a

growl of anticipation, I tear down her pants and her underwear, tug them over her bare feet, then grab her and lift her into my arms. Slamming her back against the stone wall, I hold her steady and lower her onto my waiting cock. She slides onto me with ease, gasping as I fill her up. Her legs tighten around my waist, and I use the wall to steady her so I can hold her hands up above her head.

She fixes her eyes on mine and keeps them there. I watch her face as I plunge up into her, then tilt my hips to find an angle that makes her cry out. Still, she holds my gaze.

A tsunami of pleasure floods my muscles. I try to slow down, try to prolong the inevitable, but when she whispers, "Fill me up. Show me how much you missed me," I explode. I shudder and slam forward, pressing her hard against the cave wall. I kiss her collarbones, then her breasts, then pull out of her cunt and drop to my knees in front of her.

"I need to clean up," she says, combing her fingers through my long, loose hair.

"You need to let me worship you," I growl, nudging her legs apart and bringing my tongue to her swollen clit. As soon as I start to suck on it, she holds my head and grinds forward into my mouth.

I find the right rhythm, the one that makes her start to mumble and pant, then increase the pressure. I sink two fingers inside her, then a third, then hook them forward until she shudders with pleasure.

I work her with my fingers and my tongue. I love that I can taste myself on her. She is mine again, and she always will be. Suddenly, I find it; the right combination of pressure and motion to bring her to the edge. She slams both hands back against the wall behind her. Her knees buckle, and she cries out as her hips jerk forward. I don't stop until she shakily puts her hands on my shoulders and sinks to her knees.

We are both on the floor now. Her face is flushed, her body beaded with sweat. Sparks flutter in the air around us. She strokes my beard, kisses the spot below my left ear, then leans into me. I wrap her in my arms and hold her close.

For the first time in what feels like forever, I can breathe again.

27

SAM

I peel my eyes open and dull gray light filters past my lashes. Everything hurts. Every millimeter of skin, every crevice, every cell. My hands are stiff. I almost expect them to creak when I move them. Something rough is beneath my hands. I curl my fingers into it and realize it is sand. Half-sand, half-dirt. I groan and turn over onto my back. I stare at the sky for a moment. It is a murky shade of blue. Early morning, clouds are obscuring the sun.

Slowly, I heave myself up into a sitting position, then flop forward. I rub my knees, and my thighs, trying to wake them up. This can't be a memory; it is completely alien to me. I have never been to this place before.

The sound of rushing water, tumbling down over slick rocks, makes me look up. A lake is in front of me. To my right, a tall powerful waterfall juts out from a cliff. Where it meets the surface of the lake, white foam bubbles and swirls.

Somehow, I manage to clamber to my feet. Pine trees surround the lake and curve behind me, thickening as they become a forest. Their smell reminds me of the cabin, which reminds me of Nova.

I thump my chest hard as if the gesture might psychically shake her face from my heart. It is too hard without her. Too hard and too lonely.

I look down at myself. I am wearing the same clothes I wore when I was taken from her—a black t-shirt and black jeans. They are torn now, slashes in the knees, and across my stomach.

Beneath the gaping sections of fabric, my skin is surprisingly intact. But I feel as if I am wearing a thousand cuts.

"Hey! Down there! Don't move!" A distant voice floats toward me. I search for its owner but find none. It came from somewhere above the falls. I'm certain of it.

I walk slowly in the voice's direction, even though it told me not to move. But then suddenly I fall to the ground. I feel invisible restraints tighten around my ankles. My arms are flung back, and my wrists are bound behind my back.

I don't fight it; there is no fight left inside me now. Instead, I sink to my knees and wait for my next punishment to reveal itself.

28

LUTHER

By the time I reach the lake, I'm holding fire in both hands. I don't know how the shield was breached—perhaps whoever the fuck is down there was here before we cast the incantation—but I know they can't stay.

I emerge from the trees ready to take down the stranger in our midst. Then I stop dead. My mouth drops open.

Kneeling on the grassy sand, head hanging low, clothes torn to shreds is... Sam?

I extinguish my flames and jog over to him. Kneeling in front of him, I reach for his face and turn it to mine. "Sam?" I search his features. Dark curly hair, stubbled jaw, ridiculously good angles, and—peeking out from his torn t-shirt—the silvery scars that tell the story of his years at *Spine*.

"Luther?" his voice is hoarse like he's been sucking on ash for the past few days. He frowns at me and moves as if he's trying to reach out.

I release the restraints, and he rubs his wrists. Then he holds out a shaking finger and uses it to trace the contour of my face. "Luther? This isn't a memory. It can't be." He looks around. "I've never been here before."

With no idea how to answer him, I stand up and yell at the top of my lungs, "Mack! Get out here!"

I don't know why I'm calling for Mack instead of Nova; perhaps because he might be able to tell me what the fuck I'm looking at; if it really *is* Sam. Plus, I know his bear hearing will catch my voice over the sound of the falls.

When he appears, as soon as he sees Sam, he runs toward us. With wide eyes, he looks from Sam to me then back again. "What happened?" He touches Sam's face and shoulders. "How is he here?"

Sam stumbles to his feet. I offer him a hand and steady him as he asks, "Is this real? Am I back? Are you real?"

For perhaps the first time in all the years I've known him, Mack is speechless. He rubs his beard, then shakes his head. He paces a circle around Sam, looking him up and down. Then he meets my eyes and says, "What did Tanner do?"

"I have no idea, but we have to tell Nova."

Mack doesn't reply.

"We have to tell her, right?" I ask, Sam still leaning heavily on my arm.

Before Mack can answer me, a shrieking sound comes from the direction of the caves. Nova has spotted us. She stands close to the falls, their spray peppering her face and hair. Then she runs.

Sparks fly from her skin and float up into the air as she hurtles toward us. She barely looks at Mack or me, just throws herself at Sam. Letting go of me, Sam wraps his arms around her and holds her close.

"Sam?" She steps back, shaking her head, drinking him in. "How? How is this possible?" Tears well in her eyes, then spill over onto her cheeks. "You're here? You're really here?"

Smiling a small smile, Sam says, "Seems like it."

"We have to show Tanner." Nova grabs Sam's hand and pulls. "He has to know what he did."

"Tanner?" Sam asks, frowning.

"He jumped across *dimensions* to get you back." Nova is grinning. I don't think I've ever seen her look so happy. "He did it. He brought you back to me."

Sam allows Nova to hook his arm around her shoulders and help him toward the falls. Mack and I follow close behind them. I glance at him. His eyes are flashing with their familiar amber glow.

"What are you thinking, Professor?" I ask him.

"I'm thinking that was too fucking easy," he replies.

29

NOVA

Kole has placed a pan of water in the fire and is spooning coffee into steel mugs. Tanner yawns and nuzzles into my shoulder. He seems better this morning, although I feel like he knows I'm watching him.

"Sugar?" Kole asks, looking at Tanner.

"I'm sweet enough," Tanner quips.

The warmness between them makes me sigh contentedly, but as soon as the feeling settles in my stomach it is replaced by something else. Something darker, and grittier, and more painful.

Because today, I have to make a choice. We know now that Sam is still alive. We *think* he's trapped in the underworld, The Shadow King's hell dimension, the demon realm. But we have no idea how to reach him or how to bring him back.

Tanner wants to jump again. It would mean drinking more of my blood, but that's not what worries me. It's what Kole told me about what it might do to Tanner if he keeps pushing himself.

So, it seems I have to decide... do I risk one boyfriend's life to save another?

Kole hands me a mug of coffee. Our fingertips brush against one another, sending a pulse of electricity through my body. Part of me is still mad at him, but a bigger part knows there was no way I could stay mad any longer. I need him like I need oxygen.

I'm sipping my drink, staring into the flames that warm us, when I notice Mack move from his position by the cave's entrance. He disappears quietly but purposefully.

After a few minutes, when he hasn't returned, I put down my mug and follow him. He's not in the cave behind the falls, so I step outside and follow the rocks until I'm standing to one side of the waterfall itself. A light mist sprays my face and arms. My hair is becoming damp.

I spot Mack in the distance, then Luther, then...

My breath solidifies in my chest. I can't move, or think, or speak. My body starts to shake. Every muscle contracts.

"Sam..." I breathe his name. It is like honey on my tongue. Then I run. I didn't even know I could run this fast, but I do. I hurtle toward him and fling myself into his arms without stopping to think about whether he's injured or just plain imaginary.

When I stand back and take in his face, his eyes, his thick curly hair, I know he is real.

Luther and Mack are staring like they can't believe it either. But he's here. He's really here.

I hook his arm around my shoulders and steady him as we walk slowly back toward the caves. We are at the entrance to the falls when Sam whispers, "How long have I been gone?"

"Only a few days," I tell him, turning to look up into his deep dark eyes. "But it felt like a lifetime."

Sam's lips twitch. Not into a smile, more like a grimace. "For me too," he says. "For me too."

Inside, Kole is standing up as if he was expecting us. Tanner is lounging by the fire, drinking his coffee, and flicking through his phone. "Shit," he says, eyebrows tweaking toward his hairline. "Looks like Annalise kept her side of the bargain. Nova's blood tests were leaked. The SDB hasn't commented yet, but surely this means Nova is off the hook? If people know she was human when she attacked Johnny, she'll be off the hook, right?" He pauses and looks up.

When he sees Sam, he drops his phone. It clatters on the cold cave floor. He jumps up and backs toward the wall, clutching his head. "Fuck," he breathes. "Fuck, fuck, fuck. No. Come back, Tanner. Come back." He's shaking his head, and his arms are trembling.

Kole strides toward him and grabs his shoulders. "Tanner, it's okay. I see him too."

Tanner blinks up at Kole, then glances at Sam. "You do? You really see him?"

"He's here," I say softly, bringing Sam closer. "I don't know how you did it, Tanner, but you did it. You brought Sam home."

* * *

SAM LOOKS around the cave with wide eyes. He winces a little as he takes in the fire, then shakes his head. "I need air," he says. "I can't be in here. I need air." Then he pushes past Mack and Luther, and stumbles back outside.

When I move to follow him, the others look like they're going to come too, but I tell them, "Let me speak to him alone. We have no idea what he's been through."

"Alone? I don't think that's such a good plan, Nova."

Luther crosses his arms in front of his stomach. "At least one of us should be with you."

I'm lingering by the entrance to the tunnel that leads to the front cave, itching to keep Sam in my sights because it feels too impossible that he's back. "Why?" I frown.

"Because, exactly as you said, we don't know what he's been through," Luther repeats my words back to me and suddenly I understand what he's saying; we don't know if Sam can be trusted.

I press my lips together and bite the inside of my cheek. "Alright." I nod and beckon for Luther to follow me. He grabs a bottle of water, presumably for Sam, and stays close to my heels as I exit the caves.

Sam is back on the beach, leaning forward onto his thighs and taking deep gasps of air. Luther hands him the water, and he shakily unscrews the lid. He takes several large gulps, then wipes his mouth with the back of his hand. "Thank you," he breathes. "I needed that."

Gesturing to the overturned tree trunk, I walk Sam over to it and we sit down. Luther remains a few feet behind us like a bodyguard, leaning against an upright pine.

Over the falls, the sun is creeping higher into the sky. A small slash in the clouds exposes a whisper of pale blue that promises a brighter day ahead.

I am trying to keep my emotions locked inside; seeing Sam for the first time after twenty years apart was one thing. Seeing him now, after watching him slip away from me, is altogether different. There are so many things I want to say to him. I want to touch him, stroke him, make sure he's real. I want to ask him what happened, what he saw, and if he's okay. I want to ask him how he got here.

But instead, I sit silently and wait for him to make the first move. When his fingers gingerly find mine, my breath catches in my chest. They curl around my hand and squeeze. "I was in hell," he whispers. "I mean, I think I was. I think I was in hell."

I stare down at our hands.

"I saw him. The Shadow King." He falters over his words and clutches his stomach with his free hand. "He showed me the worst parts of my life. Again, and again, and again. I thought I'd never escape." Fat, heavy tears roll down Sam's cheeks. I leave the tree trunk, kneel in front of him, and cup his face with my hands.

"You're safe now. You're here with us."

Sam stares down at me. "None of us are safe, Nova," he says, turning to look at Luther.

"What do you mean?" Luther asks, moving out from the shadow of the pine tree.

"Eve opened a portal. Her hand was there, right in front of me. She cut herself, and the blood allowed these *beasts* to cross over. Huge, gray things. Like wolves, but not wolves."

"The hellhounds," I say, locking eyes with Luther.

"It sounds like it," he replies. "Sam, what else did you see? You saw The King? Did he show you how is he planning to return to Earth?" There's a note of hopefulness in Luther's voice. We've always known what the King wants, we've just never known how he intends to get it. Perhaps this is why Sam needed to return—so he can tell us how to beat The King and fulfill the prophecy.

Sam flinches when Luther says *The King*. He shakes his head. "That was all I saw," he says. "We were in some kind of hall. The King was there. He summoned the hounds, then opened the portal." He pauses and meets my gaze. "When the hounds jumped through, he said their job was to—" He trails off, scraping his fingers through his hair. He rolls his tongue around his mouth like he's fighting the urge to vomit.

"What? Their job is to what?" Luther asks, even though I'm pretty sure we both know the answer.

Sam closes his eyes and then quietly says, "He sent them to kill Nova. He told me she'd be joining me soon."

30

KOLE

"I don't trust this." Mack puts his hands into his pockets and shakes his head. "I don't trust *him*."

Tanner still looks shaken. Every so often, he glances furtively around the cave like he's expecting monsters to jump out at him. When he saw Sam, it was as if he'd seen a ghost.

"Tanner?" I ask, putting my hand firmly on his shoulder, hoping it might ground him. "Did you see anything when you jumped that made you think you'd pulled Sam back out with you?"

For the first time in a long time, when Tanner looks at me, his eyes are swimming with vulnerability. "No," he says quietly. "I couldn't even say for certain where he was." His head ticks to the side. He screws his eyes shut, then swallows hard. "He looks normal, though, doesn't he? He looks *okay*?"

I glance at Mack. "He looks okay but—like the professor said—I'm not sure I trust it. It seems too easy. Too fast."

"We should go out there." Mack gestures to the cave's entrance, then strides outside while Tanner and I follow behind him.

On the beach, Nova, Sam, and Luther are talking in hushed voices. Seeing us approaching, Luther leaves the others and walks over. His hands are in his pockets, his expression pinched with concern. Looking at each of us in turn, he says darkly, "He's seen The King. He's been in his presence."

Mack is staring at Sam. He sniffs the air and isn't even subtle about it. "He smells different," he says. Then with no warning at all, he shifts. Nova realizes what's happening and looks around as if something terrible must be approaching through the woods and Mack is preparing to fight it off.

Snow's shoulders ripple as he huffs out large snorts of air and stalks toward Sam. Nova stands up slowly and reaches for Snow. "It's okay, it's Sam."

Snow ignores her. Actually, he barges past and nudges her out of the way. She pulls at his shoulder, but he doesn't move an inch. He is staring at Sam, his huge bear snout hardly a millimeter away from Sam's face.

He sniffs, drawing air deep into his flared black nostrils.

"What is he doing?" Sam asks, leaning back, staring at Nova. "Can you tell him to stop?"

Pushing Sam out of the way, Nova swaps places with him so she's directly in front of Snow. "Snow, stop it," she barks, as if she's reprimanding a naughty dog.

Snow refuses to look at her.

"He thinks Sam smells different," I explain, watching with slight admiration as Nova stands face-to-face with a polar bear and doesn't even flinch. Of course, he'd never hurt her but he's still intimidating as hell.

"Of course, he smells different," she says, pressing her palms against Snow's chest but failing to move him. "He's been trapped in another dimension."

"It's more than that," Tanner says quietly, putting his hand on my forearm as he moves toward Snow and Nova. His head jerks to the side. He screws his eyes shut, then pushes his fingers through his hair. When he opens his eyes again, he points a shaky finger at Sam. "I see something else."

"What do you see?" I ask, ducking to meet Tanner's eyes.

He swallows hard. "A shadow. A shadow inside him. Flickering." He shakes his head and steadies himself on my arm. "I'm not sure. I can't catch hold of it."

Sam scrambles to his feet and waves his arms. "Guys, I swear to you. I'm here. It's me. I was in that *place* but then I was here." He turns to Nova. "I told you everything I remember. You have to believe me."

But before he can finish speaking, Snow lurches for him. In one swift move, he nudges Nova out of the way, knocks Sam to the ground, then sits next to him and pins him down with his heavy white paw. Looking over at me, he lets out a noise that's half-growl, half-yowl.

"I think Baloo disagrees," Luther says, tilting his head to take in Sam's face.

Hearing his nickname, Snow snorts and turns his head away, but he doesn't take his paw from Sam's chest.

"Stop this." Nova steps into the middle of us. "He's been through enough." She turns to Snow and puts her hands on her hips. "Let him go, Snow. Please, let him go."

Snow, however, dutifully ignores her.

"Nova..." I put my hand on her shoulder, but she shrugs away from me. "I think what Tanner and Snow are trying to say is that Sam might have come back different, and that we should ask some questions before we let him close to you."

Her eyes flashing, Nova shakes her head at us. "We've been through this before, haven't we? With Nico. You judged him before you—"

"Not a great example, Nova," Luther says—more gently than I'd have expected. "We were right about Nico."

She opens her mouth to object but, before she can,

Tanner says quietly, "What happened to Nico?" He walks over to Sam and crouches down, ignoring the fact Sam's struggling against Snow's foot. "What happened to your brother?"

Nova jerks toward them as if she's going to tug Tanner away but I stop her. "He's searching Sam's emotions." I meet her eyes. *Trust him, Little Star. They're just talking. Let them talk.*

31

MACK

Sam is not himself. He smells different. Acrid. Like sulfur, and darkness, and death. Even the wolf in him is drowned by it. I sense it, and Snow smells it, and there is no way in hell we are letting him near our girl.

We press our paw hard on his chest. Not hard enough to break his fragile body, but hard enough to keep him where we want him. He writhes against us, but he cannot overpower us.

Tanner seems to have pulled himself together and walks slowly over to crouch beside us. He catches Sam's gaze and reaches for his hand. "What happened to your brother, Sam?"

We feel the boy tense beneath us. His entire body stiffens. "He was bleeding," he says. "I think he's dead."

"When did you last see him?" Tanner asks, putting his hand on the side of Sam's face so he can keep it turned toward him. We have seen Tanner do this before—he is searching Sam's mind. He can sense others' emotions easily, without needing to try, but what he's doing now is a little different. It is more purposeful, more determined. He is looking for something out of place. He's looking for something that will tell him whether Sam really is himself.

"I don't know. I don't remember." Sam shakes his head. "He was bleeding. I bandaged him." He looks down at his shirt and tilts his head. "I used my shirt..." He frowns. "But I'm wearing my shirt..." He screws his eyes shut. "I don't know," he says again. "I don't remember."

Tanner watches him closely. He moves his hand from Sam's face to his chest. Too late, we realize what he's trying to do.

He's going to jump.

* * *

I SHIFT BACK and grab Tanner's shoulders but he's already jumping, muttering quickly under his breath. His eyes are filled with the same bright white light we saw yesterday. This time, lightning does not flow from his fingertips, and he does not float in the air. He falls back and starts to shudder.

"He's having a seizure," I yell to the others. "Hold him still!"

As Sam stares wide-eyed, Luther and Kole run to us. Kole gently holds Tanner's head while I hold his upper body and Luther slams an instant restraining spell on Sam's legs and arms.

"What's happening to him?" Nova falls to her knees next to Tanner. "What's happening?"

"He tried to jump. Tried to get inside Sam's head." As the convulsions slow, I release my hold on him. He starts to cough. He has bitten his tongue and spews blood-laced saliva onto the sand. Disorientated, he struggles to sit up. Kole pulls him to his chest and holds him still. At first, he strains against him, then gradually he is back, staring at us, his pupils impossibly wide.

He finds Nova's face, then looks quickly to Sam. "It's him," he says. "It's Sam. But there's something else in there."

"What do you mean, something else?" Nova moves closer and puts her hands on Tanner's thighs. "What did you see?"

"I didn't see anything. I couldn't jump into his head because there was no room for me." Tanner takes a shaky breath. "There was no room for me because something else is in his head already."

32

NOVA

"Something else?" A shudder grips my shoulders. "What kind of something else?"

Tanner shakes his head. "I don't know. All I know is that it's nothing good."

"It makes sense..." Mack almost seems more curious than anxious. "The hellhounds were able to cross over because they're not from either world. The King could have sent something back with Sam for the same reason."

"You're saying I have a demon in my head?" Sam strains against Luther's restraints. "Don't you think I'd *know*?"

"Not unless it wanted you to," Mack says.

"But why?" Sam meets my eyes pleadingly. A jolt of sympathy makes me cross my arms over my stomach and hug myself.

"To kill me," I tell him. "Isn't that what you said the hellhounds were meant to do? Kill me so he can cross over?" I shake my head, a completely inappropriate bubble of laughter catching in my chest. I scrape my fingers through my hair. Hot tears are flicking in my gut. A wisp of smoke floats up from my skin. Sorrow and grief are turning rapidly to anger. I'm angry that I allowed myself to feel so happy. And angry that nothing can ever be straightforward, and even angrier than I might be forced to say goodbye again.

"Nova," Mack says, sending a cool breeze to kiss my skin in an attempt to calm the smoke. "We can figure this out. It will be alright."

Sam is on his knees, his feet and wrists still bound by Luther's magick. Staring at me, he says, "I would never betray you. Never. All I wanted was to return to you, but I'd never have agreed to this. I'd have suffered for a thousand years if it meant I could keep you safe." He turns to the others. "Kill me," he says, his words landing like daggers on my skin. "Kill me now before I can harm her." He jerks forward, fixing his eyes on Luther like he knows he'd be the one to do it.

"Wait," Mack says, looking at Luther as if he's worried he'll actually obey Sam's plea. "That doesn't have to be the answer. We don't know *what* is inside of you, Sam, and we don't know how long it will stay dormant. We have time. If Nova is in danger, we will protect her. But for now, we have a chance to fix this."

I screw my eyes shut and turn my back to them. I'm struggling to keep my emotions in check. It's too much. All of it is too much. "I can't do this," I whisper, unfolding my arms and letting them hang loose at my sides. "The four of you need to fix this because I can't. I can't listen to it, and I can't watch it. I can't stand around waiting to find out if Sam lives or dies or for whatever is in his head to snap." My lower lip starts to wobble, and I bite it hard in an effort to stop the tears I know are building inside me. "I spent years with an abusive man. If Sam... I can't..." The words won't come out. I want to tell them that it will break me if *Sam* is the one who puts his hands on me—if Sam is the one who tries to cut, or burn, or hurt me.

Breathing a fragile breath that makes my shoulders shake, I walk away. I'm a few feet from the rocky path that leads behind the falls when I realize Luther has chased after me.

"I want to be alone." I don't look at him, just concentrate on pressing my body to the slick rocks and moving slowly past the rushing waterfall.

"Okay," he says, inching along next to me. "Sure, you can be alone, but I have to come with you."

My eyes flash hot as I turn to glare at him. Water splashes my face, but I don't wipe it away. "Would you have done it?" I ask. "Would you have killed Sam if Mack hadn't told you not to?"

Luther's jaw twitches. "No," he says. "But if there comes I time when I need to, in order to keep you safe, I won't hesitate."

I expect anger to burst like fireworks from my skin but searching Luther's face, I see a sincerity that simply makes me sigh. I turn away from him and continue toward the back of the falls but as I hurry, desperate to be inside, and warm, and safe, my foot slips.

Luther catches me, ducks into the entrance of the cave, and holds me still. "You can't be alone right now," he says. "But I'll keep my distance. I'll stand *way* over in the corner of the cave. I promise." He's trying to make me smile, but I can't. Because none of this is funny. Not one bit of it.

* * *

FOR WHAT FEELS LIKE HOURS, Luther and I sit in silence. I stare into the flames, close enough to feel their heat on my skin. I keep waiting for the fire's sting to offer me some release—like it did when Luther used it to play with my body—but it doesn't. I reach out, let it lick my fingers, wave them through the dancing warmth, but no release comes.

Luther watches me intently but doesn't tell me to stop. Once or twice, the flames flare and send a flurry of sparks into the air around us, but I don't know which one of us is responsible.

When he finally speaks, he asks if I'm thirsty.

"No," I reply. "Thank you."

"Hungry?" he asks, taking a protein bar from the backpack next to him and waving it at me as if a slab of dry sugary oats might tempt me to say yes.

I shake my head.

Luther drums his fingers on his knees, then stands up and walks over to me. "How long are we going to stay in here?" he says. "It's a little dark, and a little depressing."

I narrow my eyes at him. "I'm staying in here until they've fixed Sam," I tell him. "If you're finding my company depressing, feel free to leave."

Clicking his tongue on the roof of his mouth, Luther sighs and sits down next to me. After a stretched pause, he says, "I told you what happened to my family."

I close my eyes and inhale a deep breath through my nostrils. "Yes, you did."

"So, you know I mean it when I tell you that I understand loss."

I hold the air in my lungs for a moment before releasing it, then turn to look at him. "I know," I whisper, tucking my arm in his and finding his hand.

"We all do. All five of us." Luther stares into the flames. "Kole lost himself when he went undercover with the League, Tanner lost his parents—even though they're still here, Mack lost Layla, and Sam lost you." He rubs his head with his spare hand then sighs. "Then in Thessaly's vision, we *all* lost you. It was Ava, but it was you. We felt the anguish, the pain, the heartbreak." His voice falters, and it makes me squeeze his hand. He regains his composure and says, "I know it doesn't help, but what I'm trying to say is that we understand. You've coped with more than any twenty-five-year-old human should have to cope with."

"I'm not human anymore, Luther."

"Except, you are. Your experiences are human. You grew up believing you were human, and now you've been thrust into a world you don't understand and given powers you can't control." He glances at me and smiles solemnly. "That's a lot, Nova. You're allowed to freak out about it."

I run my hand up his arm from his wrist to his elbow, then rub his shoulder. "Thank you."

Luther leans down and slowly presses his lips to mine. He gently bites my lower lip, then sucks it between his teeth. He cups my face with his large, strong hands, and sends his tongue to stroke mine. When he pulls away, I am flushed and breathless. "But the time for freaking out is over," he says.

I frown at him and sit back a little.

"There isn't time for it," he says calmly. "The others might not want to be the ones to say it, so I'll say it for them. This is happening. The King is preparing to rise, and *you* are the only one who can stop him. So, we need to park the freakout and go help the others. Right now."

I blink at him, both shocked and not at all shocked that he's speaking to me like this; just because he's admitted he's in love with me doesn't mean he's had a personality transplant.

Luther stands up and offers me his hand. I stare at it for a few seconds, then push myself to my feet, deliberately not accepting his help.

"Pep talk well and truly received," I tell him, pushing back my shoulders. As we pass through the tunnel and enter the cave directly behind the falls, I add, "Luther?"

"Yeah," he replies huskily.

"Next time, send Tanner for the emotional support, yeah? You suck at it."

"Yeah," he chuckles, "I know."

33

SAM

For at least an hour, judging by how far the sun has moved in the sky, the others have been debating the best way to find and destroy the demon they *think* is living in my head.

I trust Tanner implicitly. I'd trust him with my life, but I'm having trouble understanding how he can have seen a demon lurking inside me when I can't feel or sense its presence at all.

I *should* feel it, shouldn't I? The way I feel the wolf part of me? I carry its energy with me all the time. It's different for werewolves than it is for other shifters—bears, panthers, and dragons have two consciousnesses living inside one being. Us werewolves are what we are whether we're in wolf or human form. We are one, not two, but I still feel the beast part of me. The part with heightened senses, and animal instincts.

So, I should know if something foreign was in there. I should sense that something is wrong. But I don't; I feel normal. Hungover from the trauma of living through some of the worst moments of my life over and over again. But normal. I certainly don't feel like I have a parasite in my brain waiting to take over and force me to kill Nova.

"That's settled then," Mack says firmly. "We'll try the revealing spells. All three of them, and if they don't work, we'll talk to Nova about—"

"Talk to Nova about what?" Nova appeared as if from nowhere. None of us heard her approaching down the beach, but now she stands in front of us with her hands on her delightfully round hips.

Without hesitating, Kole says, "If the revealing spells don't work, we may need to ask for your help."

"What kind of help?" She looks at each of us in turn. As I watch her, I realize some of her fire is back, and it makes me smile. Seeing her broken and vulnerable, especially when it's because of me, is too painful.

"We'll explain if the spells fail," Kole says, fixing her with a dark stare.

I expect her to object, but instead, she nods and says, "Okay." Then she folds her arms. "Are you going to do the spells here?"

Glancing at our surroundings, Mack nods in agreement. "I think it's best. Out here, Kole has access to the forest if he needs it and Tanner has the lake."

I study Tanner's face. He still seems incredibly shaken. I want a moment alone with him almost as much as I want one with Nova. Not because I want to hold him close and tell him I love him—those mutterings will be reserved only for Nova—but because I want to thank him for putting himself at such great risk to try and find me for the *second* time.

"Luther, do you remember the incantation?" Mack asks.

"I remember," Luther replies. "Had a good professor, didn't I?"

A smile twitches on Mack's lips, then he says, "Alright, Sam, we need you to sit in the center of our circle. We're going to cast the incantation. If the monster in your head shows itself, we may need to restrain you, but we won't hurt you. Right now, we're trying to find out what's in there. That's all."

I moisten my lips and try to look confident as I say, "Sure. Okay."

Positioning myself cross-legged on the sand, I wait while the others encircle me. They're about to join hands when Nova nudges Luther and Tanner apart and says, "No room for me?"

They look at her approvingly and move aside to let her sit down.

"You don't need to chant," Mack tells her. "Just join hands with Luther and Tanner. You can help us channel our energy."

Nova nods then cocks her head from side to side.

"Ready, Sam?" Mack asks.

I tell him I am, even though I have no idea what I'm supposed to be ready for. Then the four guys start to chant. It's a language I've heard before but one I've never been taught to understand. Their words tremble as they fill the air. My eyes widen as flickering blue symbols appear in front of me, floating, circling my entire body. One of the symbols lands on my hand. It burns and makes me flinch. The second is hotter, the third so hot I cry out.

As the others continue to chant, I try to bat the glowing symbols away, but they rain down on me like molten rain. It becomes too much to bear. I'm about to stand and run when I notice two vines snaking toward me from the forest.

Kole's eyes are dark. He has let go of Mack and Luther's hands and is curling his fingers to bring the vines into our midst. They loop around my ankles and hold me still as the symbols multiply and beat down onto my skin.

Then there is silence. The chanting stops, even the sound

of the falls and the wind in the trees seems to have disappeared.

Mack moves into the middle of the circle and kneels in front of me, then he presses his palm to my forehead and yells something I don't understand. He tips his head back and closes his eyes.

For a trembling moment, everyone waits, staring at Mack and me.

Finally, I tentatively ask, "Is something supposed to be happening?"

Mack's eyes snap to mine. "Do you feel anything?" he asks, taking his hand from my head.

"I feel kind of itchy from all the sparkling symbols. But aside from that?" I shake my head. "Sorry, guys. I feel nothing."

With a frustrated growl, Mack moves back to his place in the circle. He breathes in deeply, centers himself, then says, "Next spell. Ready? Go."

This time, when they start chanting, the air darkens, clouds roll in, and thunder ripples through the sky. Their eyes turn black, their voices deepen. I wait for pain, but none comes. Once again, nothing happens.

The third and final spell is more dramatic still, but with the same anticlimactic conclusion. Mack holds his hands on each side of my head and screams at me. His eyes flash amber. He presses his forehead to mine and chants furiously close to my face. It starts to rain. The heavens open, and slanting stripes of water beat down on us, pummeling the lake's surface, the beach, and our skin.

But still, nothing happens.

I feel the same as when we started.

"The moon be damned," Mack curses, standing up and pacing away from me with his hands braced on the back of his head.

"Shit," Tanner mutters.

Kole shakes his head and scrapes his fingers through his long, loose hair. "I was certain the last would work," he says.

"Maybe we just need to try again?" I offer because I know what our next option is, and I truly can't bear the thought of it.

Facing the lake, Mack shakes his head. "I'm sorry," he says. "I don't think trying again will have a different outcome."

"Which means we're at the needing my help stage?" Nova asks, a vulnerability returning to her voice.

"I'm sorry, Little Star." Mack helps her to her feet and stares down into her face. "We can't allow Sam back into the fold until we're sure it's safe."

"But the voice said we need him." Nova looks pleadingly at Mack. "If we're going to fight The King, we need him. I know we do."

"I agree," Mack says. "Which is why we need you to help us persuade the demon to show itself." The professor closes his eyes and sighs heavily. "If I thought there was another way—"

"How?" Nova asks, drawing herself up so she looks a little taller and a little fiercer. "How can I coax it out?"

"You need to attack him," Kole says, standing so he's towering over both Nova and Mack. "Use your powers. The ones you used on the hounds, and the werewolves, . . . and Johnny," he adds cautiously.

Nova frowns. "No," she says, shaking her head. "That's ridiculous. I can't. First of all, those powers only come to me when one of us is in grave danger. Secondly, I can't hurt Sam. I just can't."

"You won't," Mack says. "It won't have to go that far."

"Then why—?"

"Because your energy, your power, might just wake the

demon up. Bring it to the surface." Kole nods at her like he's trying to will her to understand.

"But you're guessing," she says. "You don't *know* what will happen. You're just guessing. Even if it does show itself, what then? How do we separate the demon from Sam?"

I look up at Mack and Kole. Nova has a point; we haven't discussed this part. But then it dawns on me—they're not certain they *can* separate me from what's in my head. They need it to show itself so Nova knows they have no choice but to kill me. They need it to show itself, so she'll forgive them for what they have to do when it does.

"A spell," I say quickly, standing up and firing Mack a knowing glance. "They have a spell, but they can't use it unless the demon unmasks itself. Right?" I look from Mack to Kole, then at Tanner and Luther.

There's half a second of silence, in which we all come to understand what's about to happen, then they nod and say, "Yes, a spell."

A flutter of relief lights Nova's face. She trusts them to tell her the truth, but I hope they're smart enough to fake a spell that goes wrong rather than letting her know we betrayed her.

If she finds out, she'll never forgive them. And I can't bear the thought of her being alone and broken, facing The King by herself, trying to save the world without a cocoon of love to lose herself in when the going gets tough.

"Alright," she says. "But someone needs to help me do this because I have no idea where those powers come from or how to access them. I've only just got the hang of conjuring flames when I want them."

"We'll help." Luther jumps to his feet. "It's in there somewhere, Little Star. We just need to find it."

34

NOVA

Luther stands behind me and puts his hands on my shoulders. Sam is in front of us. The others are curved behind him in an arc formation, ready to cast their spell if I manage to tempt the demon to show itself.

"When you killed Johnny, we weren't in danger," he says darkly. "Remember? We were nearly free, running out of the building. He was no threat to you or to me, but you found your powers and used them to destroy him."

I swallow hard and close my eyes. I can still hear the sound Johnny made when he exploded. I can still feel chunks of his flesh landing on my skin and smell him in my hair and on my clothes.

"What happened when you looked at him?" Luther asks. "When you saw him in the stairwell, what happened?"

"He spat at me," I whisper, eyes still closed.

"And what did that make you feel?"

"Angry." I flex my fingers at my sides. "I felt really fucking angry."

"What did you see?"

"I saw him burning me." I drag my hand across my chest.

"I saw him cutting me." I move my fingers to the scar on my upper arm. "I saw him cursing at me, yelling at me, kicking me."

"What did you feel?" Luther's hands apply a little more pressure to my shoulders. They are hot, and their warmth spreads down my arms into my hands.

"Fear, humiliation, anger." As the heat in my arms intensifies, images from my past move like a tsunami through my head. Johnny's face, Johnny's fists, Johnny's flickering delight when he made me scream.

"Nova," Luther whispers, "open your eyes, you're doing it."

I keep my eyes closed and hold my arms out to my sides. I can feel the fire coursing through me. I feel the energy building. "Turn around," I say loudly. "Sam, turn around. If I see your face, I won't be able to do this."

I wait several beats, heat juddering in my chest, air pressing down on me.

"Open your eyes, Nova." Luther squeezes my shoulder again, then steps away.

When I look up, I see Sam's back. I narrow my eyes, encouraging my vision to blur until it could be anyone standing in front of me. It could be Johnny. It could be Ragnor. It could be Kayla.

I roar at the sky and splay out my fingers. Flames burst from the ground and encircle Sam, but he stands motionless.

The same energy I used to obliterate the wolves and Johnny is churning in my stomach. Petrified I might not be able to keep it at bay, I channel it into more flames and send them into the nearest tree. Its branches catch alight. Then I notice that Sam is moving.

"Don't…" I tell him. "Don't let me see your face."

But he keeps turning. By the time he's looking at me, his face is no longer his own. His eyes are black. His jaw stretches and clicks like a python trying to eat a fox. "Fire Bird," he hisses, his voice dripping with venom. "Fire Bird, you are mine."

He strides toward me, his skin moving like there are beetles living beneath it, his entire body jerking and jittering and clicking as he moves.

He walks right through the flames. When his arms catch fire, he doesn't blink.

"Come to me, Phoenix. Let me taste you." He flicks out his tongue, then lunges for me. He is almost on me when a rushing sound fills my ears.

A huge curl of water knocks Sam from his feet and sends him hurtling into the trunk of the tree I set on fire. He rises to his feet with ease and fixes his eyes on me again, but Tanner darts between us.

I hear Mack tell him to stop, but Tanner doesn't listen. He closes the gap between him and Sam in seconds then slams his hands onto either side of Sam's head.

"Tanner!" I yell. Looking desperately at the others, I cry, "Stop him! He'll get himself killed!" But Luther grabs hold of me and pulls me back.

With a bone-rattling scream, Tanner's arms start to shake. Black smoke curls around his hands like it's leaving Sam's body and entering Tanner's. It winds around Tanner's arms and his neck, then snakes into his mouth.

Watching it, a hot ball of nausea jumps into my throat.

But Tanner lets the smoke inside. He keeps taking it until Sam falls to the ground and the smoke disappears, then Tanner presses his fingertips to his own head, roars, and sends a plume of blackness up into the sky.

The black smoke hovers, swirls, and moves like it has a mind of its own. Instinctively, I jerk free from Luther, run to Tanner's side, and unleash the swirling hot anger from my stomach.

I reach for the smoke, splay my fingers, and scream until it explodes.

* * *

As I drop to the floor, fighting to catch my breath, the sky brightens. The sun peaks out from behind a cloud and casts sparkling reflections on the lake's surface. The falls seem louder, even the breeze feels warmer.

The tree I set on fire is now just smoking. As I watch, the smoke stops entirely. Its branches are blackened, and its needles crisp. Kole strides over to it, places his palm flat on the trunk, and chants until color returns to the tree's limbs.

Luther helps Tanner to his feet. Mack helps Sam.

I watch the five of them while on my knees, chest trembling, struggling to understand what just happened.

When Sam staggers over to me and falls from Mack's grasp, he pulls me to his chest and holds me so tight I can barely breathe. Shaking, I sit back and stare up into his face. *His* face. No demons. No monsters. "We did it," I laugh, a smile stretching my lips. "We did it. We got you back."

Sam turns and opens his arm to beckon Tanner into our embrace. He sinks down slowly, and we wrap him in our middle. Sam kisses my lips, then Tanner's forehead. "You saved me," he mutters. "For the second time. You risked everything for me."

"We should go inside. You need to drink, eat, and rest." Mack puts one hand on my shoulder and one on Tanner's.

Looking up at his friend, Tanner says, "Do you mind if we do that out here?" He glances at the bright blue sky. "I need to be in the light for a while."

"I'll fetch the supplies." Luther nods at Tanner. Mack offers to help, and so does Kole.

Whether it's because they need a moment to themselves,

too, or because they've sensed that Sam, Tanner, and I have things we need to whisper to one another, I don't know. But I am grateful.

Alone with the two of them, I take them over to the tree bench by the water and sit with my back against it. Tanner rests his head on my chest. Sam rests his in my lap. I close my eyes and feel them both. Here with me. Safe. Together.

"No more drama for a while, please," I whisper. "Even just a few days would be nice."

"No more drama." Sam hums as I stroke his face.

"Suits me just fine." Tanner kisses my collarbone, then rests a hand on Sam's shoulder while he slips the other around my waist.

We are asleep before the others return.

35

SAM

We stay on the beach all afternoon. It is a strange atmosphere. At first, apprehensive. As if we're all waiting for something terrible to happen. When Luther breaks out a whiskey bottle, however, the mood lightens.

We're all shaken, and tired—especially Tanner and I—but we're also happy. Deliriously happy.

"Maybe this is why we needed you back," Nova says as she paddles in the shallow of the lake. "Because it showed me how to access my power."

"Could be," Tanner says. He's swimming, and it's obvious that the water is helping ease his head. "Personally, I'd have preferred a less traumatic way for you to learn—"

"Yeah," I agree. "If you could have figured it all out without me having to quite literally go to hell and back, that would have been swell."

"Stop complaining." Nova reaches down and flicks water at me. "We brought you back from the dead, what more do you want?"

"Nothing," I reply, smiling at her. "This right here is perfect."

As Nova announces she's going for a swim and takes off her pants, Tanner meets my eyes. He can tell I'm thinking about my mother, and the look in his eyes makes me almost afraid to ask whether Ragnor succeeded in his plan.

I will ask. I *need* to ask. But not now.

Right now, I am going to watch Nova stripping off and submerging her beautiful body in the crystal-clear waters of the lake because—by some miracle—I'm alive. And even if it's just for a few hours, I'm going to enjoy it.

As Nova takes off her bra and makes a splash jumping in after Tanner, Mack settles next to me. "You okay?" he asks, a smile twitching on his lips as Tanner tries to convince Nova to go further out and she reminds him she can't swim.

"I will be."

"If you're not, you know you can talk to us." Mack pats my back with an open fist.

"I know." I glance at him. Quietly, I add, "Don't ever tell her, Mack."

He doesn't look at me; his eyes are fixed on her.

"Don't ever tell her there wasn't a spell. She'll never forgive us for lying to her."

"I won't," he says. "But that will be the only thing we lie to her about. Agreed?"

I nod and push my fingers through my hair. "Agreed."

Behind us, Kole says gruffly, "Who wants pancakes?"

"Pancakes? Out here?" I ask.

"It's literally the only thing he can cook," Luther says, rolling his eyes. "So, yeah, of course he brought pancake supplies to a cave in the forest."

"From a box?" Mack wrinkles his nose.

"Yes, Mack, from a fucking box. Unless you're volunteering to go to the store for eggs, flour, milk, sugar—"

"If someone's going to the store, we need more booze." Luther waves the whiskey bottle at us. We've only had a few sips each and it's depressingly empty.

"No one is going to the store," Mack growls. "We're in hiding, remember?"

Taking in his grumpy big-brother expression, I start to laugh.

In the water, Nova and Tanner have stopped splashing one another and are now kissing. *Boy* are they kissing!

He's kissing her like he's going for an Olympic medal in how to turn your girlfriend on using only your lips. Tilting her head back, she offers him her throat and grins as he drags his tongue in swirling patterns over her skin.

He's lifting her arm, kissing the soft spot inside her elbow, when she meets my eyes. Squeezing my shoulder, Mack mutters, "Why don't you join them?" But I'm already tugging off my pants.

Ditching my torn shirt, I keep my boxers on and wade into the water. When Tanner sees me, he grins, and lifts Nova into my arms. I sweep her wet hair from her shoulders and take in every inch of her face.

"I never thought I'd see you again," I whisper, tracing her jawline then tweaking her chin up so I can nibble her lower lip.

Sweeping her tongue over my lip in return, she runs her fingers over my shoulders. In the water, my scars glisten. She lowers her head and kisses the biggest, most twisted scar on my chest. Then Tanner is behind me, and he's doing the same; tracing the contours of my past with his tongue.

As Nova moves her mouth to my nipples, the jolt of pleasure that shoots down my spine surprises me. "Do that again," I whisper.

She obliges, swirling even harder while Tanner plants both hands flat on my hips and moves closer.

While I'm still in my underwear, Tanner is naked. I can feel his erection pressing against my lower back, and I want to reach for it, but to do so would mean not touching Nova.

Bringing her to me, I hook her legs around my waist. Although we're in the water, we're not too deep, and I'm standing with both feet flat on the sandy lake floor. I widen my legs and steady myself as I tease a wet nipple with my index finger.

Nova smiles and holds on to my shoulders, then she moves her head and kisses Tanner so close to my ear that I can hear their tongues caressing one another. They're still kissing when Tanner's hands find my boxers and tug them down over my hips.

I groan and lightly bite Nova's shoulder as Tanner runs a long lithe finger from my balls to my ass. He stops when he reaches my tight, un-fucked hole, and I realize that Nova is watching my face. "What is he doing to you?" she asks, then she snaked her hand around my waist, finds Tanner's, and grins. "Do you want him to fill you up?"

I swallow hard. Tanner's hot breath is on my shoulder. Fuck, yes, I want him to.

Before I can reply, he takes his finger away, spits on it, then returns it to my ass. He gently strokes my tight, waiting rim, then whispers, "Tell me if you want me to stop," and eases a finger inside.

At first, I tense. He stops, lets me adjust to the new sensation, then goes a little deeper. "Fuck," I whisper, holding tight onto Nova. "Fuck, that feels good."

Reaching her hand between us, Nova finds my cock and wraps her fingers around it. As she and Tanner find their rhythm, I wind my fingers into her hair and stare into her eyes. "I don't think anything has ever felt this good," I groan. But then Tanner adds another finger to my ass, and I almost choke on my words.

Tanner is still fucking me with his fingers when Nova slides onto my shaft and hums with delight. I try to concentrate, try to find her clit and make the small torturous circles I know drive her crazy, but the feeling of Tanner playing with my ass while Nova grinds onto my cock is too much.

"Don't hold back," Nova whispers.

Behind me, Tanner suddenly stops moving. I grind back onto his fingers, wishing there were more and that it was his cock inside me instead, but knowing that doing *that* without some kind of lube would be crazy.

Then, holy stars, he finds my prostate and rubs against it. At the same time, Nova lifts herself off my cock and replaces her cunt with her hand. She stares at me as she finds a rhythm that makes me groan. Squeezing the head with every upward movement, she cups my balls with her other hand and strokes the spot just beneath them.

"Switch places with me, Little Star," Tanner says over my shoulder.

I shudder as he takes his fingers from me, but then Nova is there instead and her fingers feel different. Smaller, more delicate. "Is this okay?" she whispers.

I can't answer her, just punch the water and moan as Tanner takes hold of her hand and shows her what to do. "Tease him," he whispers. "That's it, Little Star."

Then he disappears. He dives beneath the water, and I have no idea what the hell he's doing until suddenly there is a mouth on my cock. He's underwater, sucking my dick.

"He can hold his breath for a really long time," Nova whispers, curling her fingers in a way that makes shockwaves of pleasure course through me.

As Tanner licks and sucks my shaft, and Nova continues to torment my ass, waves of electricity shake my body. I spill hot cum into Tanner's mouth. I have no idea if he swallows it or lets it drift away in the water, but when he comes up for air, I kiss him hard.

Tanner grins and ruffles my hair. "Next time, it won't just be my fingers in your ass," he whispers, as he moves around me and grabs Nova. Scooping her into his arms, he carries her into the shallows, then lays her down in the sand. Water laps their bodies, and I watch as he holds her arms above her head, hooks her legs around his waist, and thrusts into her.

She closes her eyes, then looks up to see Kole, Luther, and Mack watching from the shore. They don't interrupt, and they don't jerk off, but they are transfixed by her.

When Tanner flips her over and pulls her up onto all fours, I expect one of them to give in. But they don't, they just lock eyes with her and watch as she strums her clit while Tanner pounds into her from behind.

When she's close to her climax, she bites her lower lip and her knees start to wobble. Tanner holds her up with one arm and braces the other on her shoulder then, almost at the same time, they release cries of pleasure and collapse into a heap.

Watching from nearby, Mack gives them a moment to lie in each other's arms then helps Nova to her feet and offers her a blanket. She leans into his embrace, and Luther throws Tanner a blanket too.

I watch as the four of them settle around the fire. Nova is in Mack's lap, giggling as he tells her she's fucking beautiful when she comes. Kole is flipping packet-mix pancakes in a small frying pan, and Luther is lacing six mugs of coffee with the dregs from the whiskey bottle.

"Sam?" Nova calls, waving at me. "Are you coming for food?"

A lump forms in the back of my throat. No matter what happens next, in this moment I am truly happy. And I will never forget it.

36

NOVA

We are back in the caves, and I am in the middle of Sam and Tanner struggling to sleep. They are both curled around me, Tanner's head on my stomach, Sam's is on my chest. I stroke Tanner's hair as he breathes deeply. Then I look down at Sam's face.

I can't believe he came back to me. It might have been a trick, but the trick backfired. I got Sam back. I have my fated five, which means we still stand a chance at stopping The King from returning.

Outside, the sound of the falls intensifies and I realize it's raining. Sliding from between Tanner and Sam, I pull my sweater on and pad barefoot outside.

The reflection of the moon—round and bright—shimmers on the surface of the lake. Rain punctuates it, making satisfying sounds as it meets the water. I sit just inside the first cave, peering out from a sheltered pocket at the side of the falls so I can see the lake and the trees.

I rub my arms as a shiver snakes down them. The rain intensifies. It reminds me of the sudden shower that pummeled the street the first night I arrived in Phoenix Falls.

I close my eyes and remember seeing Kole through the rain. His broad Viking frame, his dark hair, his hypnotizing tattoos.

The vision I saw then—hands, lips, bodies, heat—returns to me and I sigh as it fills my thoughts. I still can't tell if it was Kole I saw or the others too, but I know how it felt; like I suddenly knew myself and knew I was capable of feeling so much more than I ever had before.

As I lean back against the cool rock behind me, the vision changes. I feel my forehead crease into a frown, and my eyes twitch beneath their lids. I am seeing something else now.

The hellhounds. Flames. Teeth. Jaws. Screaming. Flames. Ash. Phoenix.

My eyes fly open. My heart is beating so fast I can barely breathe. I stagger to my feet, my legs trembling, and run from the cave. An invisible thread pulls me up the cliff toward Kole. When I find him, he is standing in the moonlight waiting for me.

You saw it? he asks silently.

"I saw," I breathe.

Without speaking, Kole pulls me to him and kisses me with a passion unlike anything I've felt before. His kiss is slow, and deep, and searching. When he stops, he presses his forehead to mine and whispers, "I'm sorry."

I stand back and look up at him. "You already knew, didn't you?" I ask, searching his face. "That's what you saw—in the woods near the commune. You saw—"

"Yes," he says. "I saw you dying."

* * *

We sit side by side for a long time, then Kole moves behind me, so I'm sitting between his legs. He nudges my sweater to one side and kisses my exposed skin, then he runs his hands over my thighs.

"When?" I ask. "Do you know when?"

"I know what you know," he says. "I know it has to happen, and I know you will return."

"Like Sam," I mutter.

"No. Not like Sam." Kole's grip tightens on my legs. "Like a phoenix. Risen from the ashes. Stronger than before. Strong enough to win."

I close my eyes and lean back onto his large muscular chest. "I'll be alone at the end," I whisper, "won't I?"

Kole breathes in sharply. The air catches in his throat as if he's trying to swallow down a clot of emotion. "I believe so, yes. But it will not be the end, Nova."

As we speak, a calmness settles deep inside me. I don't know if Kole's right. I did not see myself *rising* from the ashes. But I know in my soul that this is what has to happen.

"We should tell the others," I say, running my hands over Kole's fingers. "They deserve to know."

"We will." He tilts my chin so he can press his lips to mine. "We'll tell them at sunrise. Until then..." He hooks his fingers under the hem of my sweater and eases it over my head. "Let me make love to you, Little Star."

I don't need to say yes; he can see my desire sparkling on my skin.

For the first time since we were captured by Kayla and Ragnor, Kole takes a long time exploring my body. He caresses every inch, every secret place I didn't even know existed. He kisses the soles of my feet, my ankles, the backs of my knees. His lips and hands work together to soothe and stoke my flames at the same time. I grow hot beneath his touch, but he doesn't stop. He brings his mouth to my cunt and laps pools of arousal from my core. He watches my face when he eases his fingers into me, performing everything in slow motion—torturously divine slow motion.

When he finally enters me, I am lying on my back. I stare at the stars as he fills me as far as he can. I wrap my legs around him, angling my hips so the head of his cock puts pressure on just the right spot. I kiss his shoulders, his neck, his chest. I stroke his beard, then wind my fingers into his hair and pull his mouth to mine. I steal hungry kisses while he thrusts deeper and harder.

The orgasm that builds inside me is not a tidal wave or an electric shock, it is slow and secretive. When it finally rumbles through me, it lasts an eternity. I watch my sparks flutter up into the night sky until they become stars too, hovering above us.

I am still coming when Kole allows himself to release. He shudders and punches the ground beside my head.

"Taste me," I tell him, tilting my neck so it's close to his teeth.

He doesn't hesitate; he punctures the same fragile spot he opened for Tanner and starts to suck. The sensation of hot red liquid trickling down my neck, and of Kole lapping at my skin, makes me thrust my hand between us and circle my throbbing clit until another orgasm joins the first.

When Kole stops drinking, he stays inside me. He smooths my hair from my face, and I wipe blood from his lips with my thumb. His eyes darken, but he is still himself.

"You'll come back to us," he murmurs. "I have to believe you'll come back."

37

NOVA

At sunrise, Kole tells the others I want to speak to them outside. They emerge bleary-eyed and curious. Tanner looks better, brighter, and more like his usual self. Seeing him and Sam next to one another makes me smile.

"What's going on, Supernova?" Luther asks, stifling a yawn.

I beckon them over and ask them to sit so we are in a circle, facing each other.

Kole is next to me. His hands are folded neatly in his lap, legs crossed, betraying not a flicker of emotion on his face.

"Last night, I had a vision." I reach for Kole's hand and squeeze it because I need his strength. "It wasn't a dream. I wasn't sleeping. It was the future. I saw what will happen."

The guys look at one another. "You're sure?" Mack asks.

"Kole saw it too. When we approached the commune, he saw the same thing I saw last night. He's been keeping it from us because he had to, but I am not a seer. I can share what I know." I breathe in slowly and brace myself for what I'm about to tell them. "All this time, we've been fighting something we didn't understand. We didn't know what it truly was or when it was coming. We didn't know why I was chosen or why the five of you were fated to help me. But now I know. I know it all because last night the final piece of the puzzle slotted into place." I put my palm to my chest and press down on the tattoo that Kole inked over my scar—a moon and five planets, surrounded by swirling, intricate patterns. "Thessaly showed us that we are the ancestors of the Original Six. Their pain and their loss lay dormant in our bloodlines for centuries, waiting to be unleashed."

My five beautiful boyfriends stare at me as I speak, each one trying to figure out what the hell I'm going to say next.

"The Shadow King has been trapped in the underworld—a hell dimension he cannot escape—for thousands of years. Now, he is trying to rise. Which means now is the time for our ancestors' power to rise and help us fight him."

"Nova," Mack says gently. "We knew this already."

"But we didn't know *how* it would happen," I say. "Since the very beginning, we've been reacting instead of getting out ahead of what's going on. Bad stuff happens and we fight it off, or we run, or we hide. We've been three steps behind The King this entire time. Even when Sam went to The Hollow that night to try and stop the ritual—it simply played into their hands. Ragnor and Eve got exactly what they wanted, and we almost lost Sam."

"What did your vision show you?" Luther meets my eyes across the circle, impatient for an answer.

I glance at Kole and tighten my grip on his hand. "I need you all to promise that you'll listen to me before you freak out." They are silent, so I repeat myself. "I need you to promise."

At the same time, they mumble their promises. "Go ahead," Tanner says. "Tell us, Nova. We'll listen."

"I saw how to stop The King from returning to Earth." I look at them each in turn. "I have to die."

* * *

THERE IS a moment of quivering silence, then Luther scoffs and stands up. "No. No fucking way. This is crazy."

"I have to die, so I can return as The Phoenix."

"You're already The Phoenix," Luther snaps, fire flashing in his eyes.

"Luther…" Sam tugs Luther's hand. "We promised we'd listen. She's not done."

"Yes, she is," he bites. "I'm not listening to her talking about dying. That's the *opposite* of what the prophecy says."

"No…" Mack interrupts. He is hanging his head in his hands but looks up when he says, "It's exactly what the prophecy says. *Into the fire. One, two, three. Devoured by flame, The Phoenix is She.*"

I nod and smile sorrowfully at him. I am trying to beat down the sickening fear in my stomach and focus on what I know to be true. "In order for The King to ascend, or crossover, or whatever you want to call it, he needs my blood. That's what all this has been about. The hellhounds were supposed to capture me and take me to Eve so she can drain me. When I'm dead, he'll drink from me, and you know what my blood does." I look at Tanner and Kole. "It will give him the power to enter our dimension."

"So, you're going to kill yourself first, is that it?" Luther barks, waving his hands and shaking his head. "It's fucking bullshit crazy, that's what it is. Why would the prophecy say *fated to five* if all you need to do is jump off a cliff to solve our problems?"

"Luther," I say firmly. "I'm not going to kill myself." I squeeze Kole's hand again and he squeezes me back. "I'm going to let the hounds take me, and I'm going to let Eve drain my blood."

"Nova—" Tanner tries to speak but I hold up my hand to stop him.

"The King will drink my blood, hell will break free, and he *will* return. But so will I."

Standing up, I stretch out my arms and pull the images from my vision back into my mind. Lightning crackles on my skin. My eyes flash, and my voice darkens. "I will be reborn. The power of The Original Six will be magnified in my blood. Your love for me, with their love for Ava, and the grief you all feel will swirl, and intensify, and bring me back. And *then* I will destroy him once and for all. *We* will destroy him."

I expect one of them to speak, but they are simply staring at me with darkness and fear in their faces.

Kole clears his throat and speaks up. "If all we do is seal the portal, The King will try again, and he'll keep trying until he succeeds. If Nova's plan succeeds, he will be vanquished forever. Not for a thousand years, not for ten thousand... *forever.*"

Still, the others are silent.

My heart thuds viciously in my ears. My hands are shaking, so I lace my fingers together and close my eyes. "Kole and I both saw it. It has to happen this way. I don't want to leave you all. I don't want this to be the way it happens, but it has to. We've seen it. I have to die." I open my eyes again and draw in a deep aching breath. I try to steady my breathing and center myself. I draw my shoulders back and tilt my chin up. Then with more confidence than I really feel, I tell them, "The only question now is whether the five of you can give me one last beautiful day before the end? Or if we're going to spend it arguing about something fate has already decided." I tilt my head and start with Luther. "So, what'll it be?"

38

LUTHER

I'm so livid, I can barely breathe. I yell at the top of my lungs and send two swirling balls of fire out across the lake.

A solemn silence hangs over the others while Nova waits for her answer. I turn away from her, and I'm about to pace into the trees when Kole catches my arm.

"You'll regret it if you don't do this with her," he says, meeting my eyes. "It has to happen, Luther. Arguing or running away won't change it." His voice falters a little, and I notice that his big Viking hands are shaking when he strokes his beard. "The best thing we can do is give her the day she asked for. Spend the next twelve hours together, then..." He trails off.

"How?" I turn back and interrupt what Nova's saying to Tanner. "How will it happen?"

She stares at him for a moment, then sits down and the cold early-morning sand. I hesitate before following suit. Kole stands behind her, hands on her shoulders, like a fucking sentinel, like it's his responsibility to remain stoic, and calm, and devoid of emotion.

Nova slides her hand into mine. Over the past few weeks, I've grown used to how warm she is. No other woman has ever run hot enough for me; even other fire witches feel cool to the touch. But Nova *is* fire. She's the warmth I've needed my whole miserable life, and she's telling me the conclusion to all of this is that I have to say goodbye to her? I stare at our entwined fingers. A lump of emotion settles in my throat.

"I'll go to The Hollow. I'll make them think I'm there to kill Eve, but I'll let them capture me." She looks around at the rest of us. "The five of you have to stay away. You can't come with me."

I shake my head, almost laughing. "So, we just wave goodbye? Sit here not knowing what the fuck happened?" I search her face, hoping she can see from my eyes that this is killing me too.

"You can watch from the woods if you have to," she says softly. "But I need you safe. All of you." A smile lights her lips. "I need you here when I come back."

"We will be." Mack sits up on his knees in front of her. He strokes her hair from her face and kisses her forehead. "We'll be here, Little Star."

Tanner looks away. He rubs his temples and exhales a long, shaky breath. The emotion in the circle must be killing him, and he has his own to deal with too. But then his face changes. Like he's locked it all away, he smiles. He's carefree Tanner again, and he stands up offering Nova his hand.

"The answer is yes," he says to her. "If this is happening, then *yes*, Little Star, we will give you your perfect day. So, what do you want to do first?"

Nova smiles up at him, then wraps her arms around his waist and leans against his chest. Tanner's brightness falters for just a second as he kisses the top of her head, but when she looks up at him, he raises his eyebrows and says, "Well? What'll it be?"

Wiping the moisture from her eyes, Nova turns and looks at Kole. "Got any more of that pancake mix?" she asks hopefully.

Kole clears his throat, dislodging whatever emotion was sitting there and says, "You're in luck. One more box."

"Then I'd say coffee and pancakes is a pretty good start," she replies.

Nodding at her, Kole stalks off to fetch the supplies. Mack follows him, but I remain with the others. Tanner and Sam have cocooned her, like they can't stand *not* to be touching her. They're stroking her arms, her fingers, her hair. She closes her eyes and turns her face to the slowly rising sun, absorbing their touch.

Usually, this kind of touching would lead to sex. But right now, it's not about that; it's as if they're trying to memorize every inch of her.

"I'll be back," I snap, then I turn away and stalk into the trees. Under the shadow of the ones closest to the lake, I lean my forehead against a trunk and breathe in the heady scent of the pines. I clench my fists then unclench and brace my palms on the tree. I can't do this. I can't lose her. Not when it took me so fucking long to admit I needed her.

Okay, she says she'll come back. But do we really trust that? I know the others do; Kole, Mack, and Tanner have believed unwaveringly in the prophecy from the very beginning. Sam probably believes it because he managed to return, so why can't she?

But I've always preferred facts over faith, and there is nothing—*nothing*—that tells me witches can rise from the dead. Returning from a hell dimension? Okay, sure. Being *reborn* after your heart stops beating? That's a different thing entirely.

Kole's words ring in my ears. *"It has to happen, Luther.*

Arguing or running away won't change it. The best thing we can do is spend the day together."

I turn so my back's facing the tree then sink down to the ground and clutch my head. I don't know how the others are doing this. I don't know how the others are staying so strong because I feel like I'm falling apart.

I'm staring at the ground when something catches my eye. A thick piece of wood, perhaps broken off when Nova threw fire at the tree yesterday. It's strangely shaped, and curled a little at the end.

I look from the wood to my hand. My vision blurs. I see myself standing in a chapel with Nova in front of me. I see us exchanging wedding rings.

I know it wasn't us. I know it was our ancestors, but I remember how it felt to be her husband. I remember how it felt to know that she was truly mine, that I was truly hers, and that nothing could break us apart. Even death.

I pick up the wood, take out the knife I've been carrying in my pocket since we arrived, and start to carve.

39

NOVA

Luther misses breakfast. Kole calls him, but he doesn't emerge from the woods. Mack offers to go after him, but I tell him not to. "He needs some time, it's okay."

While we eat, I feel like the others are forcing themselves to look like they're enjoying it. I can hardly blame them; I'm asking a lot. Perhaps too much.

Eventually, I put down my little silver camping dish, drink the last of my coffee, then say to Tanner, "We never did have that swimming lesson. Will you teach me?"

He hesitates for a moment before smiling and saying, "Sure, but this time no funny business. It's serious stuff, I want you to concentrate."

I nod and mock-pout at him. "I promise."

When I follow him into the water, I warm it with just a click of my fingers, and it's like we're wading into a hot bath. Sam joins us, but Kole remains on the shore with his coffee.

I look for Mack and realize he's removing his clothes. I drink in the sight of him, memories flashing in front of my eyes. Then he shifts, and Snow comes ambling toward us.

"Snow *loves* to swim," Tanner says as the polar bear wades with ease into the lake and swims out to its center.

Sam follows Snow, and the two of them lark around in the deeper water while Tanner starts by teaching me how to tread water.

We stay in the lake most of the morning. Eventually, Kole joins us, and I don't think I've ever seen anything as hot as his half-naked Viking frame striding into the water. When his long dark hair gets wet, I realize I'm wrong. *Now*, he's the hottest thing ever.

Kole is holding my waist, wrapping my legs around his middle, when Luther emerges from the trees. He stands, watching us for a moment, then Kole says, "Maybe we should dry off?"

I unhook my legs from him and follow him as he wades back onto the shore. The others join us. When he reaches the sand, Snow shakes himself all over then turns effortlessly back into Mack. We grab blankets from the pile Kole and Mack brought from the cave and wrap them around ourselves.

"If only we had hot chocolate," I mutter.

"Coffee will have to do, I'm afraid, Little Star." Kole sets the silver camping kettle into the middle of our little fire, then sits down and gestures for me to sit between his knees.

Wrapping his blanket around both of us, he kisses the spot below my ear. I'm about to turn and kiss him when I realize I need to pee. Jumping up, I tell him I'll be back, and head for the trees to relieve myself.

I'm only gone a minute or so, but when I return the guys are talking in hushed voices. They look up when they see me. Frowning at them suspiciously, I scoop up my clothes and tug them on. The guys do the same, none of them speaking.

Finally, I put my hands on my hips and say, "What the heck is going on? Are you plotting to kidnap me and stop me from going to The Hollow?" I laugh a little, trying to make light of the situation. "Because I could take you all down. You know I could."

Luther is the first to step forward. Before I realize what's happening, he takes my hand and folds down onto one knee. I blink at him, utterly confused.

"Luther, get up," I hiss, but he simply stares up at me.

"Nova," he says, his breath catching in his throat. "I have never loved anyone the way I love you. Never thought I could." His eyes flicker a little as he tries to jokingly add, "Especially a human."

Tears have sprung to my eyes, but I have no idea why. I laugh and wipe them with the back of my free hand. "I love you too."

Luther reaches into his pocket and opens his palm. Inside sits a small wooden ring. Not glossy or polished, but beautiful all the same. He lets go of me and picks up the ring, holding it with his thumb and forefinger. So solemnly it almost makes me giggle, he meets my gaze and says, "I pledge myself to you with this ring. Will you accept it?"

A heady mixture of overwhelming love and emotion swirls in my chest. Is this a mage tradition or is Luther just making this up? Whatever the answer is, I know *my* answer straight away. "Yes," I whisper. "Of course, I will."

Luther presses his lips to my knuckles, kissing them gently, then slides the ring onto my left hand. My ring finger. Where an engagement ring would sit. I stare down at it before he stands, sweeps me into his arms, and kisses me.

I'm still giddy when he steps away, and I realize Sam is now the one kneeling in front of me. I look around at the others. Holy hell. They are *all* holding small wooden rings.

"It has always been you," Sam says, his deep dark eyes staring up into mine. "I pledge myself to you with this ring. Will you accept it?"

I nod, unable to speak. As Sam slides his ring onto my little finger, tears start falling. He stands, cups my face, and kisses the tears on my cheek. Then lets Tanner take his place.

Looking down at Tanner's floppy hair and wide smile, I can't help laughing. Before he says anything, I wiggle my hand at him. "I accept," I tell him. "I really, fucking accept."

Tanner's ring fits my middle finger. When it's firmly in place, he picks me up and whirls me around. "You're a terrible swimmer," he mutters, "but you've been my girl since the moment I set eyes on you." His finger brushes the ring he gave me. "Now, you always will be."

For some reason, when Mack sinks to the floor at my feet and holds out his offering, chills snake up and down my arms. Seeing him like that—vulnerable, opening his heart to me—makes me want to fall into his arms and never leave them. "You reached a part of me I thought was lost forever," he mutters, brushing his lips across my fingers. With a knot in his throat, he manages to say, "Little Star, I pledge myself to you with this ring. Will you accept it?"

I nod, unable to reply, and offer him my hand. He slides the ring onto my index finger, kisses it, then stands and pulls me to him. Tucking my head under his chin, I breathe in his scent and the feel of his warm arms encircling me.

Then he joins the others, standing in a semi-circle behind me. And it is Kole's turn.

He looks down at the ring in his hand but remains a few paces away from me. I stand with my arms at my sides, watching him. Images flash through me. That first night in the rain, and all the times after. "Little Star," he breathes as he closes the gap and bends his knee in front of me.

"Kole..." I smooth my palm over his long dark hair, then cup the side of his face. He closes his eyes and leans into my touch.

You have always been a part of me. You will always be a part of me.

I shiver and take his hand. When he opens his eyes, he whispers, "Promise you'll come back to us."

I nod, tears running in rivers down my cheeks now. "I promise," I reply.

"Nova," Kole says. "I pledge myself to you with this ring. Will you accept it?"

Barely able to breathe, I reply, "Of course, I do."

He stands and tucks his finger under my chin, turning my face toward him so he can kiss me gently on the lips. Then the others are there too. My five fated mates, bound to me forever.

For a long time, the six of us kiss, and touch, and whisper all the ways we love each other. When I next look at the sky, the sun is dipping lower over the falls.

It is nearly sunset.

It is nearly time.

40

NOVA

When we let down the shield and leave the falls, Luther allows the fire to go out. The beach falls into a dim half-light. I stare at it for a moment, then look down at the wooden rings on my hand. One for each digit, one for each of my mates. I run the fingers of my right hand over my left.

The others are stoically silent. Pain is already etched on their faces, causing ominous flutters of doubt to settle in my chest every time I look at them. Even Kole, who has perfected the art of being the strong silent type, is rattled.

"You saw it too," I say quietly as we turn away from the falls and start our journey through the woods.

"I did," he replies.

"It's not forever. I'll come back to you."

"I know." Kole brushes his fingers against my elbow. We have left our packs behind—because there is no use for them where we're going—and yet we're not holding hands.

A little way behind me, Sam and Tanner are walking beside one another. Mack's jaw is so tightly clenched, I'm surprised he hasn't given himself a migraine, and Luther is barely able to speak to me.

He's not angry anymore. At least, I don't think he is. He's always been hard to read, and the fact he's told me he loves me hasn't made it any easier.

We walk until it is pitch dark and stars have replaced the clouds and the birds. A sheet of silence has fallen over the woods. Even the breeze has slowed to barely more than a whisper.

I breathe in the scent of the pines and stop when we reach the edge of the woods. We are about to emerge on the road that leads up toward The Hollow. Without looking at the boys, I say calmly, "Wait for me at the falls."

"Wait for you?" Mack moves into my eyeline. He's frowning, and his eyes are dark.

"I'm not sure how long it will take me to come back." I meet his gaze. "But you can't stay near The Hollow, it's too dangerous. Wait for me at the falls. I'll come to you there."

Mack glances at Kole. My Viking nods in agreement. "We will wait for you at the falls. We won't leave until you return," he says.

"You might need to detour for pancake supplies," I tell him, trying to muster a smile. "It could be a few minutes, a few hours, a few days... I have no idea."

Kole tries to smile back but seeing his lips curve makes me frown. "I like you better when you're grumpy," I tell him, nudging his ribs with my elbow.

"Speak for yourself," Tanner says, hooking his arm around my waist and squeezing it. "It wouldn't hurt him to be just a *little* less grumpy. Just a little."

For a moment, all six of us laugh. But it's not normal laughter; it's nervous, unnatural, and makes my stomach clench with sadness.

Turning to face them, I fold my arms, then unfold them, then fold them again. "It's time for me to go." My voice is shakier than I want it to be. "You need to wait here. I can't put you in danger."

"No way." Luther strides forward and grabs my hand, showing me my own fingers. "What we said to you when we gave you these rings... it was a solemn vow, Nova. Not a game. We are yours. You're ours. And we will *not* let you do this alone."

I expect tears to bite at my eyes, but they don't come. Perhaps I'm stronger than I realized. "I wish you could be with me at the end—all of you—but I can't risk your lives. I need you here so I can come back to you. If I return and you're gone—" I shake my head. "We will win this fight together, which means the five of you need to stay safe."

"I will go." Kole's voice is strong and firm. "I will watch from the trees. I'll stay until the end. I won't let her out of my sight."

Luther and I start to object at the same time, but Kole simply clenches his fists at his sides and stares at me until I stop talking.

"I will go with you. The others will wait here." He meets my eyes. *Let me do this for you, Little Star. And let us both do it for them.*

Finally, I nod at him. "Alright."

Mack kisses me first. A deep, searching kiss. Like he wants to commit the feel of my lips to his memory forever.

Sam's is slower and more tentative, Tanner's urgent—like what he's feeling and what I'm feeling will overwhelm him if he stays close for too long.

Luther is last. He runs his finger over the ring he gave me, holds it to his lips, and kisses it. But he does not kiss me. As he turns away, Tanner puts his hand on Luther's back, but Luther shrugs away and stalks into the trees.

For a moment, I watch him walk away. But then my body

jolts forward and I run after him. Grabbing him by the arm, I dart in front of him. Tears are running down my cheeks so fast I can barely even see his beautiful, grumpy face in front of me. Staring up at him, I yell, "By the stars, Luther, I love you so damn much. You have to believe me when I say that I *will* come back to you."

Luther doesn't move. His eyes trace the lines of my furrowed forehead, then he tucks his thumb under my chin and—almost angrily—brings my lips to his. When I reach up to touch his face, I realize his cheeks are wet too. For several long seconds, our lips smash into each other, searching and full of sorrow. Finally, Luther puts his hands on my upper arms and prises me away.

I am staring at him, breathless, when Kole takes my hand and gently guides me away. When I glance back over my shoulder, Luther is still looking towards the trees, away from everyone. His head is bowed, and his broad shoulders are shaking.

"You'll see him soon," Kole says. Then he puts his arm around my shoulders and guides me away.

This time, we do walk hand-in-hand. We hold onto each other until we reach the huge, imposing gates of The Hollow. Illuminated only by moonlight, the wall that separates the trees from the sweeping driveway looks taller and colder than usual.

We follow it into the trees, then reach the spot where it turns into rubble. "Was it always like this?" I ask as we stop beside it.

"For as long as I've known the place," Kole says, nudging the broken stone with the toe of his shoe.

Stooping down, he picks up a small brown leaf and blows it from his palm. It flutters in the direction of The Hollow, but when it touches Eve's invisible shield it fizzes and drops to the ground.

"You will have to make it known that you're here," Kole says. "They'll come for you."

I nod, biting the inside of my cheek.

"Are you afraid?" Kole asks, looking out at The Hollow instead of at me.

"Afraid of dying?" I shake my head. "No. Afraid of *how* they'll kill me? No." I turn and reach up to hold his face with both hands. "Afraid that I'll never see the five of you again? Yes. Terrified."

Kole presses his forehead to mine. He runs his hands from my shoulders, down my sides, to land on my hips. "You will see us again. I promise."

I wipe tears from my cheeks with the back of my hand, then breathe in deeply. "I have to do this now," I whisper, looking up at the moon. "Or I never will."

"I will wait in the shadows. I will not leave," he says solemnly. Then he says, "See you soon, Little Star," and turns away.

41

KOLE

Turning away from Nova is the hardest thing I've ever done. The bond between us hums, and stretches, and twists in my core. My blood pulses in my ears, and my throat, and my heart.

As she moves further away from me, I can still feel her breathing. The rhythm of her heartbeat is the same as my own. Then it changes. It quickens. I feel heat. *Her* heat.

When I turn, she is hurling balls of fire at Eve's shield. They are bouncing back, setting the forest alight, releasing the smell of pine and smoke into the air. I step into the shadow of the trees, and watch, every muscle in my body twitching with the need to go to her.

It takes only seconds for Eve to appear. She strides down the steps, waving her arms. When she reaches the fountain, she stops, bounces up and down on the balls of her feet, then cries, "Ragnor! The Fire Bird has come!"

At the same moment Ragnor emerges from the house, so do the hellhounds. Not as many as before—only six—but just as vicious. They scamper toward Eve, then stop at her ankles like a pack of sheepdogs waiting for instructions.

Eve says something I can't hear, causing them to sit on their haunches and lick their lips, then she strides toward the trees.

"Fire Bird," she calls. "You have returned to me. But where are your mates?"

"This doesn't concern them," Nova shouts. "I've come to finish what *you* started." She throws more fire at the shield. "When you kidnapped me and tortured me. When you tricked me into believing Nico was my brother. When you took Sam from me!"

Eve stops on the other side of the shield. The two of them are barely inches apart but cannot touch. She starts to smile. "Fire Bird, I didn't take your Sam from you. I believe that was Kayla's doing. Sadly, though, she is not here."

Nova's hands are down at her sides, bright white flames flickering inside them. But it's all for show; she's not using even half of her power, and she doesn't intend to.

For a few seconds, they stare at each other. Eve's eyes are dark, familiar black veins snaking out from their corners. She ticks her head from side to side, then reaches into the pocket of her flowing dress and takes out a small glass vial.

My mouth goes dry, and my tongue swells. She's going to take F.H.B, and I have no choice but to stay and watch.

In barely a flicker of a second, Eve downs the blood. She shudders from head to toe. The lines on her face spider out toward her neck, chest, and arms.

The fire in Nova's hands dances higher. She stretches her arms out to her sides, then braces herself as Eve lets down the shield.

Instantly, she attempts to throw fire in Eve's direction, but Eve waves her hand and flicks it away. It hits the ground instead and fizzles out.

"Is that all you've got, Fire Bird?" Eve laughs. Up above, dark clouds move across the sky and half obscure the moon.

Thunder crackles. Eve lets out a shrill squeal, then claps her hands.

Nova strides forward, but the next time she raises her hands, Eve clicks her fingers. The hellhounds come running. Nova casts a circle of flames around herself and runs.

When the beasts catch her, she screams and tries to set them alight. I lurch forward, almost too far forward. Is she changing her mind? Is she truly trying to fight them off?

I see lightning sparkle in her palm, but then she clenches her fist, and it disappears. No, she is not trying to fight them; she's trying to make it *look* like she is fighting them.

"Bring her to me," Eve coos. The hounds have their teeth clamped around Nova's wrists. Not tight enough to do what they did to Rev, but tight enough to draw blood. I can smell it. I can *taste* it in the air.

Ragnor takes the steps two at a time and stops next to the fountain. "Here," he barks. "The King said it needs to be here."

Almost singing with joy, Eve cries, "The fountain! We will do it in the fountain!"

She skips in front as the hellhounds drag Nova along the cold ground. Two holding her wrists, two at her sides, two at her feet, snarling at her ankles.

I move forward and stand in the shadow of the nearest tree. I brace my hand on its trunk, scratch my fingers into the bark, and try to breathe through the torturous need to kill every single one of them.

When they reach the fountain, Eve crouches down and strokes Nova's face. Her mouth forms the shape of the words *Fire Bird*, then she grins and stands up. She snaps her fingers and the beasts let Nova go. They've barely released their grip when Ragnor wraps his fingers around Nova's throat and hauls her to her feet. His body quivers as he stares into her eyes.

"Holy hell. Do you know how much I want to be the one to end your pathetic little life, Fire Bird?" He presses his face close to hers, then the bastard fucking licks her cheek. From her jaw to her temple, he drags his filthy tongue along her skin.

Nova doesn't flinch or close her eyes. She has done this before; she is well-versed in remaining calm in the face of an evil man doing evil things.

"Trust me," she retorts, "not as much as I want to end yours."

Ragnor stares at her, then laughs and tightens his grip on her throat. She gasps for breath, tugs at his hands, and tries to kick him. Finally, he lets go and throws her to the ground.

"Not there," Eve says. "Inside the fountain. It has to be done inside so we can capture her blood."

Nova's skin starts to smoke. Her eyes flash. When Ragnor jerks her up by her elbows, she presses her red-hot palms to his arms and makes him cry out.

Snarling, he punches her in the gut. Hard. Then he picks her up and throws her into the fountain's waterless, stone basin. Nova hits her head hard and reaches up to touch her forehead. Blood trickles from it and runs down the side of her face.

My throat constricts. This is not what I saw in my vision. I saw flames, and I saw the hellhounds, and I knew she would die. But I did not see any of this. I did not see her being beaten in front of my eyes.

She tries to sit up, but Ragnor hits her again and she falls.

He's about to unleash his fist on her for a third time when Eve grabs hold of his arm and says, "This is not what he wanted. The longer we play with her, the more chance there is of her mates coming to rescue her." Eve snaps her fingers and the hellhounds come to her sides. "We finish her. Now, Ragnor."

Ragnor's shoulders are quivering. As I watch him, I vow with everything inside me that it will be me who ends his sorry werewolf existence. I will torture him until the last pitiful breath leaves his broken body. And I will enjoy every second of it.

"Fine. Do it." Ragnor steps back.

Nova is crouched inside the basin of the fountain. She tries to press herself against the tall stone column behind her, but it's too late. The hellhounds are coming for her.

They pounce on her, six of them. Teeth, flashing eyes, and huge dripping jaws. The first to puncture her skin stops to release a howl that shakes the mansion. At first, she is silent. But when they begin to tear pieces of flesh from her bones, she screams. The sound brings me to my knees. I double over but force myself to keep watching. I told her I would be with her until the end. I told her she would not be alone.

Nova, can you hear me? We have never reached each other from this distance before but I need her to hear my voice. I need my voice to be the last thing she feels before her world goes dark.

Kole... Her reply is faint. Barely audible. But it's there.

Don't try to talk. Just listen. Listen to my voice. I'm here, I love you.

She screams again.

I'm here, Little Star. I love you.

This time, the scream falters. A hound sinks its teeth into her neck. There is the sound of skin breaking, but I can no longer see her. All I see is the arched backs of the hellhounds as they devour her.

"Enough." Ragnor looks at Eve. She clicks her fingers, and the beasts jump down from the fountain. Blood and saliva drip from their jaws. Nova's blood.

I stand up, steadying myself on the tree beside me. All I can see of Nova is her pale arm hanging over the side of the basin. My mind flashes back to the first time I saw her. The night I brought her to my apartment above The Cross when she lay on my couch with her silk-smooth arm flopping down beside her.

Now, it is not smooth. It is torn and broken. Blood runs down it, dripping from her fingers onto the grass below her, painting her rings a deep, dark red.

Eve takes hold of Nova's wrist. She sniffs it. Her tongue darts out as if she's going to take a taste for herself, but Ragnor snaps at her to, "Leave it, Eve." So, she shoves Nova's arm back down into the fountain and moves away.

"When she stops bleeding," Ragnor says, "give her body to the hounds. I will fetch vials for the blood."

Crouching down, Eve strokes the hounds' ears. "I will watch her."

"No need," Ragnor snaps. "She's dead. She won't go anywhere."

"I like watching her bleed," Eve says, standing so she can stare into the fountain.

And she does; she watches Nova until Ragnor returns, transfixed, humming to herself, stroking her own arms, and running her fingers through her long, tangled hair.

"Here." He thrusts a large glass vial at her, then takes another from his pocket. "Two will be enough?" he asks.

"Two will be enough," Eve says, picking up Nova's hand and holding it so the blood now drips from her fingers into the vial. "He only needs a few drops. But she is precious. If we can gather more, we should. The King will be extra especially pleased."

Ragnor dips his hand into the fountain to fill his own vial. "If you want more, you can go fetch another vial."

Eve shakes her head. "I can't go. I like watching her like this. I like watching her..." She stops and frowns, then she says, "Smoke."

"Smoke?" Ragnor grabs Eve's elbow. "What are you talking about?"

"Smoke...there's smoke." Eve points a long pale finger at the basin. She staggers back, clutching the vial. "Was that supposed to happen? When we drained her?"

I see it too. Plumes of pale gray smoke float into the air. They swirl around the fountain, growing faster and thicker.

Seconds later, the smoke turns to something else; flames. Flickering orange flames. At first, they are small and weak, barely more than embers. Then they grow. They surge toward the sky. They spread like wildfire, consuming the fountain.

Eve and Ragnor back away, the hounds start to howl, the flames dance higher, and The Phoenix Prophecy echoes in my head.

Devoured by flame, The Phoenix is She.

LOVE FLAMES?

If you enjoyed Flames, I would be incredibly grateful if you'd leave a review so that others can discover it too!

As an independent author, reviews are one of the most important tools we have to help spread the word about our books.

Even if it's short, it will be *hugely* appreciated.

You can leave reviews on Amazon, Goodreads, or Storygraph - just search for The Phoenix Prophecy and hit 'leave a review'.

ABOUT CARA

If you love why-choose romance, magic, super-hot mages, and even hotter RH scenes, then we're destined to be friends.

I mean it when I say I love keeping in touch with my readers. Come say hi over on TikTok.

www.caraclare.com

amazon.com/Cara-Clare/e/B09ZQRV4QG
tiktok.com/@caraclareauthor
instagram.com/caraclareauthor

THANK YOU

Thank you for reading Nova by Cara Clare. If you are looking for more books to get lost in please check out our other published titles at;

www.apbeswickpublications.com.
A.P Beswick Publications
Oswaldtwistle Mills Business Centre
Clifton Mill
Pickup Street
Accrington
BB53AP